Contents

PART THREE Departing in More Ways Than One

PART ONE

The Castle

The Dark Horn

NORA

I heard a cow lowing, lowing low on the lea—a mournful sound full of calling. It called me as I stood there at the window listening in the warm twilight of October.

Eben said, "Come to bed, Wife."

"There's a sound I hear," I said. "Ah, but it's only a cow." Yet I did not go to his side. It was more than a cow, I knew. It was more than that.

"It's the dun heifer," he said. "She'll be bulling."

"I'll just go see," I said, more to myself than to him.

He did not say anything. It might be he was near asleep already in the warm bed. And my babe, sleeping in the cradle, never stirred as I went down the stairs.

I stepped out into the dew and the deep blue light of evening. All around the farmhouse the tall oaks stood twisted, and the fir trees crowded black at the edges of the field. Far down across the meadow, the water glinted pale blue where the bay rounded the islands. I went down through the meadow. Behind me, in the dark house, my babe began to wail.

Any other night I would have turned back at the sound of

that crying. Many a time already my heart had been wrung in me by his cry—so loud a cry from so small a babe—my first baby, only four days old! But this night his cry had no power over my heart. It was the cow's lowing, plaintive and mournful, that drew me steadily down through the wet fields—down to the shore, rank and salt with the sea smell.

Low tide, the sands stretching silver-white far out into the bay. I felt nothing strange that a cow should be out there, away so far out and lost. I walked out, straight across the firm sand, hard-ribbed by the tide, where little pale silver fishes slithered and flashed before my bare feet in the few inches of water in the tidal pools. The darkness grew deeper around me, and the sands darkened along with the sky. Only the last light still held in a thin gleaming at the far edge of the sea. Soon I would be in darkness far out on the tidal flats, all alone. But the cow's calling! I could think of nothing but that mourning, that sadness. It filled my whole soul with its sorrow. A cow's lowing is a sad sound—I had always thought so—but this was more than that. There were words crying in the sound. Almost a song:

> *Come Nora!*
> *Come Nora!*
> *You must come!*
> *You must come with me!*
> *You must come nurse the Erl Prince*
> *In a kingdom low by the sea.*

It was not the cow that spoke those words. It was a small man with a horn, standing by a long black boat there at the edge of the tide. But I never knew when it was that I first saw him, or when he first spoke. The cow's lowing became the dark horn blowing, and then it was too late—if ever I could have turned back, I could no longer.

The Dragon Boat

NORA

When I stepped into the shallow water and into the black boat, it seemed that my husband, my baby, my home, and all I had left but a moment before had fallen so far away that my thoughts could no longer reach there. I stepped into the black boat, and my whole world faded away. High on the curved prow the carved dragon's head turned and flickered its tongue at me. The small man put down his dark horn, and the long boat slid out into the current and glided silently into the darkness with never a breath of wind or a sail or an oar to move her. She slipped through the black water that was so still it scarcely rippled at the boat's passing.

I remember neither fear nor wonder at the strangeness of it. I sat there quiet in the bottom of the boat among tarry ropes and other dark shapes, and I felt like a lifeless shape, as if I myself were a dark cloak wrapped around my own self.

There was no sound, only the water churning against the sides. I may have fallen asleep. I may have awakened and slept again. And even when I was awake, I lay in a state of drowsiness until sleep overcame me again. It seemed as though endless time passed, but it may have been no more than a night, for I remember starlight, darkness, and moonlight, never sun or blue sky above me. The great dragon head rose curving up black before me, cleaving the sky, and the hissing of the water under the keel was like the hissing of the dragon itself, whispering the same words as the horn: "Come Nora . . ."

I remember too that it was night when, after the long sea passage, the dragon boat first drew near to a low dark shoreline. The moon was hidden by cloud cover, but still its soft light gleamed through. As I lay in the boat, half-dreaming, I could see the shore, so black, drawing near, and even the reflection of the shore in the dark water. We sailed slowly along, following the shoreline, and the dark land mass broke apart and formed again and again broke up as we passed by many small islands, heavily wooded with black and tangled fir trees.

Then our boat turned into the mouth of a narrow channel that wound deep into a marsh, a vast grassland. The moon broke through, and its light glittered across this great sea of grass. I saw on both sides the tall stalks gleaming, the soft plumed heads bowing and waving in the breeze. It almost seemed that they were spun out of silver, for the moon's rays touched them with a cold brilliance. I stared entranced at the grasses rippling and swaying as we passed, until my eyes grew heavy and closed again. And in the dark behind my eyelids I saw the plumed grasses repeated in an endless pattern, gliding toward me on both sides out of the dark night, the water road pale before me, and the great dragon prow cleaving the center.

When I roused myself again from my sleep, I found that it was dawn, a gray dawn, barely light, and we were enclosed on all sides in a soft, luminous mist. The fog opened before us and closed in behind us as we followed a winding waterway through the tall plumed grass. I drowsed again, and when I awoke it was even lighter. But still I could see only dimly ahead, until quietly, like a frail curtain tearing apart, the fog thinned to streamers of white mist, and we were deep in an eerie, mysterious swampland.

Giant trees stood with their trunks steeped in the dark heart of the water, their branches interlaced overhead, growing so densely that they let little light fall between them. Great drooping masses of gray moss hung from their boughs and trailed across our path, so that we passed through veils of both moss and mist. Only an eerie gray twilight filtered down from the sky. It was so quiet I could hear no sound, only the lapping, lapping of water as it licked at the sides of the boat.

Then abruptly there was a clamor that shattered all the stillness: the screeching of a vast multitude of swamp birds taking off from their nests all atangle in a huge gnarled tree. Around us they flew and over us with a great wild flapping of wings—long-legged, long-necked birds, light and dark.

As the boat moved on, we passed more of these great nesting trees clotted with massive clumps of matted and snarled twigs. Often across our path the great trees had fallen, their dead branches trailing to bar our way, but always the dragon boat glided smoothly through, between, and around them. Rotted stumps, too, thrust out of the water, covered with thick green blankets of moss and with tangled masses of vipers draped over them that hissed at us as we passed, and our dragon head hissed in answer. But still I felt no fear and no wonder.

Slowly between the trees the land grew more solid but still

deep and green with moss, until we were gliding down a narrow river between two thick walls of dense forest, the trees very ancient, very huge, and moss-draped. Surely those woods were wolf- and bear-haunted, and yet we saw few signs of life. Once a herd of elk grazing knee-deep in the water raised their great antlered heads, watergreens dripping from their pendulous lips, and stared at us as we glided past.

Then at the last we sailed out from the dark tree shadows onto a great quiet lake, and, in its center, an island with an ancient fortress, a huge stone castle, moss-overgrown, with square watchtowers and high crenellated battlements. Great flocks of gulls and ravens swirled through the air, and as we drew near, I saw that on each stone of the battlement a black or a white bird perched.

The Castle

NORA

There in that great stone castle I remembered nothing at all of my life that had gone before. It was as if my mind had been emptied, drained of all memories. Like a child I saw everything afresh with a sort of innocent wonder. Yet, even then, I knew I was no child. I knew my name and how to do the simple everyday things, such as washing and dressing and eating, but little else.

I found, too, that I could not speak. I was completely mute, locked in a strange dead silence, as if someone had turned the key on the door of my speech and locked my words within. I could think and hear words, but there was no way that I could utter them. It must have been a part of the spell that was on me—a part of the forgetting.

For the most part, as I recall now, I lived in a dreamlike trance and did as they bade me. But sometimes my thoughts would struggle free and I would be filled with anguish, wondering at the place I found myself and puzzling over why I was there—though I could not think where else I should be.

As to the why and the wherefore, it should have been plain to me from the first, for almost as soon as I set foot in the castle, even before I had been given food or drink after that long sea voyage, the same small dark man who had brought me there in the dragon boat ordered me to follow him and led me up a flight of stone steps, high up to the top of one of the great towers.

The stone staircase climbed steeply up inside the thick castle walls, an almost endless flight of steps up through a dim tunnel roofed and walled with huge blocks of rough gray granite. Only thin shafts of daylight came sliding through narrow slits set deep in the thick walls. It must have been that the day outside had grown overcast, for I remember the flaming torches that hung in iron brackets at each landing. Steel-helmeted and chain-mailed guards lounged beside great iron-studded doors that led off the stairwell, and huge gray dogs there were, too, that crouched beside each doorway, growling in undertones as I passed them by.

Weary and breathless, I arrived at last at the top of the last flight of steps. There we entered past the guards and the guard dogs into a chamber hung with flowered tapestries of a lovely rose-pink hue, and more tapestries underfoot, so that it seemed as if I had stepped into a secret box lined with pretty paper. I remember that thought coming into my mind and wondering where could I have seen such a box lined with flowery rose-colored paper? I know now that it was the memory of my own sewing box, but at that time the image had no meaning and merely baffled me. Often after I first came to the castle such elusive thoughts troubled me—thoughts that seemed like dream fragments. And always I felt a sadness and a terrifying sense of loss as these torn scraps of memory drifted into my mind and passed, as a shadow passes over the sun, leaving a chill in the air.

In the center of the room that I entered stood a huge carved bed hung with deep night-blue curtains, each bedpost entwined with intricate carvings of vines and flowers, all prettily painted, and more flowers embroidered on the blue velvet hangings.

A lady lay in the bed, propped up by many soft pillows. Her hair was long—shining like a skein of light silken floss, as pale as finely carded wool, all falling about her white face with its huge silver-blue eyes. In a great carved chair beside the bed sat a man, massive and gray. He seemed one with the gray granite blocks of the castle, one with the gray guard dogs. He was dressed in a gray robe trimmed with dark fur, and about his waist a wide gold belt with a great sword slung from it. His bearded face was broad and flat, heavy-browed, with an ugliness that seemed the opposite of the lady's frail, pale beauty.

My eyes fell away from the man's fierce ugliness, but they were drawn to the face of the lady, and I gazed at her with wonder. My dark guide bowed low to his knees and ordered me to kneel to the King and Queen of Erland. I seemed even then aware of what this meant, and it filled me with uneasiness to find myself in the presence of royalty. Indeed, I felt I had no right to be in that room, but the Queen spoke kindly to me and told me to rise and come forward. She questioned me softly, "Whence have you come, Nora?"

Even had I been able to speak I would not have been able to answer, for I knew not whence I had come.

The King laughed then, and his laugh was like a hammer blow. "She'll do," he said. "She has a pretty face."

"It is not her face we need," the Queen said in a thin, cold tone

He sat there studying me. "I see nothing lacking. If my son lives, he'll enjoy a pretty face as much as his father does."

The Queen smiled wanly then and turned to my guide and said, "You have done well, Clootie. You will see that Nora is guarded well. You will watch over her and be her steward."

Then she beckoned to one of her handmaidens who stood by. The maid stepped up to the bedside and leaned over and lifted a small bundle wrapped in white. As she picked it up, it let out a thin wail of misery. The sound of it struck me and made me tremble as nothing had before.

The maid placed the small bundle in my arms and said simply, "This is the Erl Prince. You must nourish him."

And at once I pressed the small whimpering thing to my breast. I was so happy to hold that poor little thing and be able to give it my milk. Though I had no memory of my own babe, I knew what to do. And I felt that this babe needed me desperately. It had been so hungry, its little ugly face so wrinkled and gray like the face of an old, old man, and its thin arms like brittle winter twigs. But I felt love for the poor little thing almost from the instant that I took it in my arms.

"That is my son, Prince Elver," the Queen said softly, her voice full of sorrow. "Take good care of him, Nora, for I cannot." That was all she said, then she turned away her face, and it may have been that she was weeping silently.

The babe and I were taken back to a room low at the castle base, a large room that looked out into a flowering garden on one side and out over the lake on the other. A rough bare stone room, it was, without wall hangings, but with fur rugs scattered about on the cold stone floor. The room was furnished with chairs, a low chest, various small hanging cupboards, and a heavy table. There was a wide bed hung with curtains for myself and a cradle for the babe, though often on cold nights, as winter came on, I took him in my own bed to keep him warm, for he was so frail that he took chill easily.

13

Not that we were ever too cold or uncomfortable, for there was always a great log fire blazing on the huge hearth.

I had a nursemaid to help me care for the babe. She was named Menia, a large, clumsy, dim-witted girl but good-natured and very quiet. Since I had no speech there was little passed between us. But Clootie (as the Queen had called him) was always about, and his talk was enough and more than I cared to hear. He gave all the orders for food and whatever else might be needed for the babe and myself. The others called him Hjuki, but I always thought of him as Clootie, for so the Queen had named him.

I came to know him well, but I could not like him. He was an ill-natured runt of a man; that is the best I can say for him. There was little in his narrow face but mockery and malice. His hair was coal black turning gray on top, and his pale eyes caught the light and glinted like bits of ice when he made his jokes. Ay, he had a tongue as sharp as a skinning knife. He would often mock poor Menia, calling her Fousome Fug, Ugsome Ugh, or The Great She-Ox, and he would taunt her by singing:

> The eyes in her head are like two rotten plums.
> Turn her around as the mill wheel hums.
>
> The teeth in her head are like harrow tynds.
> Turn her around as the millstone grinds.
>
> The lugs on her head are as long as a mule's.
> Turn her around and she'll still be a fool!

"Move your great gowking carcass!" he'd shout at her. "Or must I take a gavelock to ye?"

It was a black wit that he had! There was a blackness about him always—his clothing as black as his nature, and a laugh like a rusty hinge creaking high at the end.

Menia would be gulping down tears, and I would be fuming at Clootie. Indeed he treated all the servants in such a mean and vicious manner that often I was enraged at him. But he would laugh at my dark looks, and then he'd turn the edge of his tongue on me.

"Why are you sulking, you poor cow?" he would ask. "You're making us all sick with your glooms. Shall I dance Hannykin Booby or Clutterdepouch to cheer ye?"

And little I knew what all that meant. His tongue drew no blood from me. I had no liking for Clootie; there were times when I hated him thoroughly, but I accepted him as I accepted all that happened to me.

Perhaps once every week or so it might be that the Erl Queen would send for me to bring the babe to her. She had been ill since first I had seen her, but she would smile and take the baby Prince in her arms and croon to him.

"Ah, how fair he has grown," she would say. "My Princeling, my bright jewel, my sweetling. My little blue-eyed lovely son!"

It was true. He had lost the ugly weazened-old-man look. He was still frail and small, but a beautiful child, with soft fair curls and a lovely smile. However, his mother would soon tire of holding him, especially now that he had grown more active and would keep squirming to be free. She would hand him back to me with a sigh, and then I would carry him back to the gray stone nursery.

Or it might be that the court physician would come to see that the babe was well cared for and in good health. He was a short dark man named Raekkin. Both he and Clootie were almost dwarfs, but where Clootie was thin and sharp-featured, Raekkin was heavyset, with a rugged, almost ugly face. He was as odd in his ways as Clootie and often gruff and illtempered, but he had a kindness under the gruffness that Clootie lacked.

I was not allowed ever to leave the room, unless escorted to see the Queen. But I might gaze out the windows into the walled garden and see the gardeners at work and the seasons changing. The flowers would bloom and fade, and new flowers would take their places. I would see fair ladies in embroidered gowns strolling there, attended by gentlemen in garments just as rich and colorful, and often the King himself might be there among them. Sometimes they would bring instruments and play sweet music, sitting about the fountain in the warm afternoons. The fountain would be sending its misty spray high into the air, all glittery with rainbow sparkles from the sun, before falling down again, splashing back into the pool there below, where carved marble figures of strange beings crouched—mermaids, sea horses, and giant frogs.

That garden was like a magic show that I might watch, but so remote and unreal to me that I neither thought nor hoped that ever I would set foot there.

On the lake side my windows looked out on a different and even more dreamlike beauty. Often boats would glide by on the wide dark lake, each frail craft gleaming with light as it swept past toward the mist-shrouded shore. Often the black water rippled and sparkled with the wind's passing, but sometimes the water would be as still and smooth as polished ebony. The boats that passed were no two alike, but all of the same type—all white, as if carved of ivory, and intricately designed. At times the structure was so delicate that it seemed like an egret's feathers or fine lace. Their shapes were graceful, with high, smooth, curving bows and with many fan-shaped sails that spread like delicate insect wings on either side. They all moved without sound, gliding smoothly past the castle, far out across the lake, until they disappeared, vanishing into the curtain of pale mist.

And my days drifted by like those white boats dissolving

into mist. Although often I was touched by a vague feeling of loss, for the most part I was content, caring for the small babe that I loved so dearly.

Yet there were other times when I would awaken in the night seized by a strange unrest, filled with apprehension and anxiety, so that I could no longer sleep. I would arise and cross the firelit floor to stare into the black mirrors of the night casements. There I would see my face staring back at me, pale, hauntingly resigned—a face that seemed always the face of a stranger, so little did I know of my own self.

The dark image of the dragon boat would sweep across my mind, and I would long to cry aloud, "Who am I? Whence have I come? What was my past life?"

But I could not cry out, and there was none to answer.

The Jackdaw

NORA

I remember how the sunlight made water shadows that flickered on the stone walls, and the swans that glided by below the windows. I would toss out scraps of bread to the birds, and my Princeling would reach out his hands to them and make calling noises.

I would be holding him tightly, letting him lean out the high, narrow window in the thick wall. In the dark lake water I would see the white swans' mirrored shapes—curved neck bending down to meet curved neck, like the white outline of a dark heart. A few soft, curled white feathers might be floating on the still water. Perhaps a fish would come up to the surface, strike at a feather, and sink down again out of sight.

So it was, as I recall, that day—I, with the babe, throwing crusts to the swans, and Clootie fishing, leaning out of the next window, whistling one of his tunes. Ah, how I hated the sound of his whistling. It was full of unpleasant notes, discordant like a crow's voice but shriller—more like a jay's shrieking. He caught a fish, like none other I had ever seen, and pulled it up flapping and slapping its tail against the rough rock wall—a large fish with jewel-like scales, as bright as a flower bed, all sparkling in the sunlight. The fish's mouth opened and closed, gasping silently.

I am like that fish, I thought. I am out of my element, too, silent and helpless. I felt the tears well up in my eyes and roll out, running slowly down my cheeks. I turned away from the window, rocking the babe in my arms.

The water lights moved and rippled across the stone walls of the room as I laid the babe in his cradle and rocked him gently. He wriggled and kicked, and I began to hum a soothing lullaby. The words ran softly through my mind. Words that seemed strange to me. I did not know where I had learned them:

> *Sing shusheen shurra lurra lay,*
> *Sing shusheen shurra loo.*

Slowly the words formed pictures in my mind, pictures of a stone house, very different from this castle. A small pitch-roofed stone farmhouse set in an autumn grove of huge trees with russet-red leaves. A long flagstone hall leading into a whitewashed room, and a red fire burning on the hearth.

More words drifted into my mind:

> *May no ill will now threaten us*
> *My helpless babe and me,*
> *Dread spirit of the wan water*
> *King Owen's wild banshee.*
> *May holy Mary pitying us*
> *For grace in Heaven sue.*

Sing shusheen shurra lurra lay,
Sing shusheen shurra loo.

My humming became as much a comfort to me as to the baby Prince. I felt a sense of peace, and yet a feeling of great loss. I felt, too, as though I could speak if only I tried. Slowly, my voice hesitant and rusty from disuse, I repeated aloud:

"May holy Mary pitying us for grace in Heaven sue. . . ."
My own voice sounded strange in my ears, but my wonder was shocked out of me by another sound—a dreadful screaming howl, like some animal in excruciating pain. It was so unexpected, so startling that I jumped up in terror. I turned to find Clootie standing there behind me. It was he who had made the sound. He stood there, his face contorted with rage, shaking with some terrible inner fury. It seemed he was about to spring at me, but he did not move, he only glowered, and his words when he got them out at last were shrill with hatred.

"You've found your voice, have you, you bitch! Little good it will do ye!" And in this strange wild anger he swung his arm and flung the fish at me. It struck me full in the face before I could raise my hand to fend it off.

"Clootie!" I screamed. "Stop it!"
And what happened next was strangest of all. There was a loud *Crack!* as if the whole room were about to break like an egg. At my feet the fish lay flapping feebly, but Clootie was gone! Behind me I heard the babe's high wail of fear. In alarm I turned to him, and as I turned I felt a great gale of wind rushing through the room and heard a shrieking and fluttering as of a multitude of birds. But I saw nothing. The sound grew, rumbling and reverberating from all corners of the room. It's an earthquake, I thought, terrified. I snatched up the screaming babe in my arms and ran to the door, but be-

fore ever I reached it, I heard a small shrill voice, and the words it spoke were so odd yet so familiar that I stopped, not believing what I had heard. Then I turned, and there in the center of the floor crouched a black bird with a gray crown and nape—a jackdaw! The words he spoke were a pitiful squawk: "Jack's a brave bird! Jack's a brave bird!" as if to assure me that he was no coward.

It was I who felt like a coward, for I was shaking all over. But the bird looked so comical and ruffled, crouching there, that I began to feel laughter rising, catching in my throat. I felt that I had known him perhaps in some other time, yet I felt too that he was no friend, any more than Clootie had been. His cold, light, glittering eye was cocked at me, the black feathers all ruffled up in fright. He seemed stunned as by a blow, hunched up and panting soundlessly. Perhaps he had flown in the window on that strange rush of wind. I had seen birds stunned so by flying into a wall.

As I stood patting the babe gently to soothe him, I stared at the bird, struggling to hold an elusive memory. I tried my newfound voice. "Jack?" I asked doubtfully. "Is it you, Jack?"

He came scuttling across the floor to my feet. He looked so pathetic that I leaned over and held out my hand, and he hopped up onto it. The babe stopped crying and reached out to pat the bird, laughing and starting to babble with delight.

It was all so strange, but no stranger than everything else. From the beginning I had accepted all that happened to me, and so I accepted the jackdaw's coming.

I could not imagine why Clootie had flown into such a wild rage or where he had gone, though I could easily understand why he had rushed away after hurling the fish at me. I had seen Clootie in a rage many times before. When he was truly furious, his mocking manner changed. He became cold and venomous, under complete control. Ah! He had a snake's heart. But this time it was as if he were in the grip of some force outside himself. He had really frightened me. I had felt for a brief moment that he had wanted to kill me—and in the end, after all, I had only been struck in the face by a wet, cold fish! Unpleasant as that was, it was still a harmless thing.

No doubt now Clootie would be somewhere in the castle feeling foolish and perhaps ashamed of his actions—if Clootie *could* feel shame, which I really doubted. I doubted he had any feelings but spiteful ones. He was so full of spite, it stuck out all over him like spines on a hedgehog. But I had never had reason before to fear Clootie. I was safe from all but his sharp tongue, because the small Prince needed me. Indeed the Erl Queen always treated me kindly and spoke graciously to me. She knew I loved her child as dearly as she did herself.

I sat holding the babe in my arms, rocking him gently, thinking happy, comforting thoughts now that we were alone. The water ripples of sunlight on the walls were so soothing, so soothing, almost like a music for the eyes. It was pleasant to be alone with the babe. The jackdaw scrabbled about the floor like a small evil spirit, pecking at crumbs, but again I had lost whatever shred of memory he had brought back to me.

I slipped my bright golden ring off my finger and strung a long ribbon through it. The babe and I watched in amusement as I dangled the ring before the bird while he tugged at it and tried to fly off with it. It was a foolish thing to do, but I had often played so with the babe and thought nothing of it.

"Ah, Jack, you were always a wicked thief!" I murmured, as I teased him with the bright ring. I wondered why I had said "always," and wondered, too, that the words I brought to mind could be spoken aloud at last. I felt as if I had shed some heavy weight that lay on me. I felt lighter and happier. I could ask questions now, if only I could think what questions to ask. I knew there were many things I wanted to know. But what were they? For the moment my mind was a blank. It doesn't matter, I thought; I can speak at last. When I have questions, I'll be able to ask them.

The babe quieted and grew sleepy. I did not put him back in his cradle, but curled up in the big carved armchair, holding him. I drew my feet up under me, tucked the cushions behind me, and leaned back, rocking him gently, laying his small head close to mine. I felt so drowsy and relaxed that my eyes closed almost before his. I let the gold ring drop and never felt it when the jackdaw tugged the ribbon from my hand.

Dream Memory

NORA

I slept, with the baby Prince in my arms, so sound, but I dreamed—oh, I dreamed! And my dreams were all of the life I had lost, things I had never dreamed of since I had come to that castle in Erland.

In my dream I stood at the door of the stone farmhouse that I knew was my lost home far away across the sea. I stepped out into the heat of the late-afternoon sun and walked across the dusty barnyard. I walked slowly toward the stable, gazing about me with delight to find myself back home, even in a dream. I felt the warm breeze twisting the loose strands of my hair, felt the warm dust through my thin slippers. Everything seemed so clear, so real—realer than real life ever is. Even smells—the sweet strong smell of cows, the sharp sour smell of pigs. And small sounds—the twittering of swallows, the sparrows' high cheeping, the low murmur of the barnyard fowl that clustered about my feet hoping for corn. I looked at my flock with delight, recognizing each bird, each favorite hen: the one with golden hackles on her dark neck; the gray penciled Brahman hen, so soft and heavy, with her bedraggled feather-duster feet; my silver duckwing cockerel! Each was so beautiful and so familiar to me. Even the five fierce gray geese bowing their long necks and raising their chins as they hissed at me. I longed to reach out and stroke the green velvet heads of the Rouen drakes, but they were none of them that tame. Eben's black-and-white collie bitch came padding across the yard, wriggling her fat rump in greeting. I knelt in the dust to welcome her, letting her dirty my clean apron with her dusty paws, and not caring. Then I rose and went on down to the stable.

Eben was there unhitching the mare, her colt trying to suckle as he undid the traces. The colt's tail switched furiously; it was so comical, so eager. I stood apart a little in my mind, watching Eben. I knew I was dreaming and knew it had been an eternity since I had seen him or thought of him. My husband! I stood watching him, his arms brown and muscular, his fingers so strong undoing the buckles of the harness. My heart felt as if a great wind of love were rushing through its long empty chambers. And then the scene was no longer a dream, but like a play I was taking part in, and I lived again my past.

Eben turned his face to me. "I've brought you a gift, Nora," he said.

"And would it be the calico I told you I wanted?"

"Calico? Now, I must have forgotten that!"

"Indeed! Would you be teasing me? But if you've forgotten, I want no foolish thing like perhaps a bunch of ribbons or a new pair of combs."

A strange high little voice behind me cried, "Awk! Awk! Jack's a brave bird!"

I jumped and looked over my shoulder, so that Eben burst out laughing. He left the unharnessing and climbed up into the market wagon and lifted down to me a large wicker cage. In it was a black bird that squawked shrilly and fluttered its black wings.

"Was it he who spoke?" I asked, half fearful, for it seemed an unholy thing, more like an evil spirit than a bird.

"You wanted a talking bird," Eben said. "There you are. You'll never find a bird any cleverer than that one! It's a jackdaw."

I took the cage in my hands, still half afraid and yet pleased, for I loved all creatures. And it was true; I had wanted a talking bird ever since I had been a little girl. My father had been a sea captain with a green parrot that sailed on voyages with him, but my mother would not have it in the house.

The jackdaw spoke again. "Heart's delight! Heart's delight!"

Truly, a talking bird had been my heart's wish! The wisdom of it filled me with wonder.

The dream scene faded and merged into another. I found I was standing in the coolness of my own flagstoned kitchen. I reached up and hung the bird cage on one of the hooks in the low ceiling. Eben was sitting at the table, where I had laid out cold meat and bread and Cheddar cheese, for I had let the fire go out on this hot day.

I went down into the coolness of the cellar to draw a pitcher of ale, and again I was struck with delight and wonder at being home. It was all so real—the cool darkness of the cellar, the damp smell of the earth floor, the pans of milk sitting cooling on the long shelf with the golden cream rising to the top, the large round cheese wheels in the screened cheese closet. I felt like touching everything. I wanted to feel it as well as see and smell it all. The two great oak casks stood side by side, one of cider and one of ale. As I bent over the spigot, drawing off the pitcher of ale, watching it foam up, I slowly ran my fingers over the smooth wood of the cask with a feeling of pure delight.

I came back up to the kitchen, and as I saw Eben at the table, the love of him filled me, so that I leaned over, placing the pitcher before him, and leaned my cheek warm-pressed close to his. We kissed and I was filled with the joy of it.

I was in Eben's arms, but somehow the scene had changed again. He was carrying me up the stairs on our wedding night, the kitchen below noisy and full of friends. There was a sudden silence, and all the faces turned toward us. Then the fiddlers and pipers started up again, and all the dancers clapped and stamped their feet.

"You'll not slip away so easy!" Eben's brother, Nat, shouted. He grabbed a saucepan off its hook and followed us up the stairs, pounding on it with a ladle. Others followed, doing the same, beating on tin pans and pails till the din was ear-shattering.

"I'll murder you—in the morning!" Eben said, as he set me down and pushed the door shut in Nat's face.

They pounded and banged away on their tin until they grew tired at last, but little Eben or I cared. Through our night of love-making the dreamlike music seemed to go on and on: first the fiddlers and dancers pounding away belowstairs till the whole house rocked like a ship; then, when at last the dancing ceased, we could hear the music change to sentimental strains. They were singing "Bonny Doon" and "Wandering Willie" and "The Flowers of the Forest."

As I lay, held close in Eben's arms, listening to the music, drowsiness was stealing over me. Someone was singing "The Castle of Dromore," and again the dream scene shifted.

I was a small girl held close in my mother's arms, sprawling half asleep in her lap as she sat before the hearthfire. Her soft sweet voice was singing my favorite lullaby, as her hands gently combed my long hair:

> October winds lament around
>   The Castle of Dromore,
> But peace is in those lofty halls,
>   My precious treasure store.
> Though leaves may fall and flowers die,
>   A bud of spring are you.
> Sing shusheen shurra lurra lay,
> Sing shusheen shurra loo.
>
> May no ill will now threaten us
>   My helpless babe and me,
> Dread spirit of the wan water
>   King Owen's wild banshee.
> May holy Mary pitying us
>   For grace in Heaven sue.
> Sing shusheen shurra lurra lay, . . .

Then in my dream it was myself that was singing this song to my own small son, as I gently rocked his cradle:

> "Sing shusheen shurra loo."

"Owen Kimbell." I whispered his name in the soft darkness. "Owen," named for my own father. My baby was asleep now, and I moved across to close the window. Far away I heard the lowing, the sad lowing of a cow. I stood there listening in the twilight.

Eben said, "Come to bed, Wife."

But all I could think of was the lowing of the cow, calling me. In my dream I left my sleeping baby in his cradle and my husband near asleep in the bed. I went down through the meadow, the wet evening grass cold under my bare feet. Behind me in the dark house I heard my baby begin to cry, but I went on, down to the edge of the sea and the sand flats stretching away silver-white far out into the bay. The lowing of the cow drew me out to where the black boat waited with the horn calling me—Clootie calling me with the dark horn, "Come Nora. . . ."

At the sight of the dragon boat, at the sight of Clootie, I froze. In my dream, I stopped and terror swept over me. The dark horn called me, called me, but somehow I tore myself free, I turned and ran back, in a dream-flight of fear, in a nightmare terror, back across the dim sands, back up through the long meadow, back into my house and up the stairs. I snatched my baby from his cradle and held him clutched to me, crying, weeping with relief, relief at my escape, relief that I still held my own baby in my arms. . . .

. . . I awoke from that dream of remembering. I awoke weeping, my eyes blind with tears. I could not stop weeping, even when I was fully awake at last, for the whole of my dream remained clear in my mind. I knew it was all true, all of it—*all except the very end*. This was the life I had lost. It had all come back to me, and the sorrow of the loss was too intense to bear without tears.

The baby Prince, the babe that was not my own, was still there in my arms, awake now and hungry, crying loudly along with me and beating his small hands against my breast, demanding his milk. I could not refuse his hunger, and I let him nurse. But as I held him the tears still fell, running down my cheeks, for my heart kept asking, What has become of my own small newborn son? How could I have left him behind? How could I?

The sun was low now, and the flickering water lights on the wall were tinted pink, deeper and deeper pink, slowly turning red, until the room was embroidered with flame, shifting and moving in waves across the darkening walls.

I sat and wept in the room that I now knew was my prison in a strange land.

The Husband

EBEN

Nora never came back to bed that night. I heard her leave the window and go to the door. I tried to rouse myself to call her back, but somehow I could not come full awake. I managed to turn over toward her, but I only saw her going, disappearing out the door, her white gown in the dark doorway and her long hair hanging black down her back.

I felt a sleepy disappointment, that was all, a sort of disgruntled feeling. Devil take her, I thought. What's she want to go off downstairs for? I heard the cow's lowing, too, a faraway sound like a horn, but it seemed nothing special, nothing to worry about. I lay there in the bed with a heaviness creeping over my limbs. It was not sleep, but a feeling of dead weight so heavy that I began to come wide awake with a sense of vague alarm. Something was wrong with me. Something was wrong! And Nora had been gone too long. I tried to rise, but I couldn't. It was as if I were weighted down, fastened to the bed. A sort of panic seized me as I struggled to free myself. I could hear my own labored breathing loud in the quiet room. The babe, too, must have heard it, for he burst into a loud wailing that went on and on and would not stop. It was more than I could bear. I tried to shout, but I could not even do that. I was held by some powerful force, helpless and silent in the bed. The feeling of helplessness had a nightmare quality.

Then suddenly I came free, as if unstuck from glue. I jumped up, staggered to my feet, and went reeling across the room like a drunkard. I ignored the babe; it was Nora I wanted to find. Something was wrong, something I could not understand, but I felt it.

I saw her trail where she had gone down through the damp meadow. The grass lay brushed aside where she had passed. It was bent all which way, heavy with evening dew. I followed down to the shore. Her footprints led out across the flats, out in a straight line to the water's edge, and the tide coming in! Terror filled me, and I ran like a madman out across the flats to the tide's edge. I waded out, calling and shouting, straining to see some sign of her, but there was nothing but the dark sea waves rippling under the low half moon.

I wanted to drown myself, as she must have done. What else could I think? There was no reason for her to walk out there, out into the water. But though I waded far out and wore myself out with calling and thrashing about, I could not let myself go to the bottom. Finally I staggered back to the sea's edge and lay there, dripping wet and icy cold, gasping and sobbing with exhaustion.

Then at last I rose and walked the shore. I walked all that night, first one way, then the other, mile after mile. I could not rest. I was searching for some sign. I did not feel the cold at all. My mind was almost numb, but I still held onto a faint hope that I would find her. Perhaps she had swum ashore somewhere. I knew she was a strong swimmer; it wouldn't be easy for her to drown herself. If I couldn't, I thought, then she couldn't. I clung to that thought, but I never found her that night or the next day. I do not know when I gave up searching, but I finally remembered Owen, my small son. I remembered Owen, and at last I went home.

As I approached the house, I expected to hear the baby screaming with hunger, but it was quiet. Was he dead? Had I let him die too? My heart sank in me, like a stone in a bottomless well, and I pushed open the door with dread. Bab Magga stood there holding Owen in her arms, her red hair falling down all tangled from the knot it was skewered in, and her dark eyes bright and excited.

"You're a fine one!" she greeted me. "Leaving your wee babe alone. If I hadn't come along, Lord knows what he'd have done. What the devil have you been up to, Eben? And where's this precious babe's mother?"

But I could not tell her. I did not know the answer.

She grinned at me, like a cat with a cream pot. "All dripping wet! And in your nightshirt too! What've you been doing, drowning your wife, maybe?"

I felt sick suddenly. "I want you out of here!" I said, but my voice was so hoarse it sounded like a thick whisper. I wanted to shout at her, but I had not the strength left in me.

"Oh no," she said. "Who'd care for the dear little boy? It was Tom Haggett came by and found your house all deserted, the little darling squalling his heart out and your stock all uncared for. Tom could take care of the stock, but he couldn't feed the babe, now could he? So he called me in. I've given the little dear three bottles of milk already, he was that hungry."

"You'll kill him," I said.

"Oh no, dear. Oh no! There's not many would know just how to mix the milk for so young a babe, almost newborn. There's none other in these parts, that's for sure. But you don't have to worry, dear love. I know how to take care of him."

The glitter in her eyes seemed to hold me. I felt like a rabbit caught and choking in a snare. My legs were starting to tremble. I sank down in a chair at the table and buried my head in my hands. I felt so sick I could not look at her.

It was the first time Bab Magga had ever set foot in my home, and that was shock enough in itself, for I'd thought I was well rid of her. There'd been a time long gone when I was but a lad and she a ragged redheaded brat taunting the boys and throwing muck at us as we passed the hovel she lived in with her old mother. We called her mother a witch, but she was a harmless old thing compared to Bab Magga. For there'd come a time when she was all at once a young woman, her temper and her hair like fire, wild and full of deviltry, with a fierce laughter and a way that could draw boys after her. She'd think nothing of dragging a boy into the bushes if she so wished, and if she didn't she'd turn on you and screech and scratch and bite and kick like a demon. She had us all set one against the other, and us blacking eyes and bloodying noses, and she'd laugh at us and not always go with the winner.

I never knew it was me she preferred over the others—not until I started courting other girls—and then she'd lie in wait for me and say, "I've a bone to pick with you!" Ay, and she'd pick it clean. She'd fair scream at me and carry on that I was slighting her. But she never made public the way she felt; it was always when she caught me alone. There were times when she could turn up sweet as honey, and sometimes she could win me over and sometimes not. It was love and hate between us from the start, or I thought it love at the time. But when I met Nora, then I found out what love was. Bab Magga had no chance with me from then on.

Now I felt as if my whole life had been turned upside down and wrecked all in one night. What was happening to me was beyond human understanding—Nora gone and Bab Magga standing there rocking my young son in her arms with that cream-pot grin on her face.

I could say it was for the sake of the babe that I let her stay. At least I thought it so at the time. I know now there was a spell that she'd laid on me from the first, and when I found her there I know now that already I was helpless against her. There was no way I could have been rid of her.

All I remember of those first days is that I was sick to my heart and fair desperate in my love grief for Nora. It did not matter a whit to me who else might be there in the house. I could not get Nora out of my mind. I hired a small boat, for I had no boat of my own then, and I spent days combing the coast, dreading I'd find her drowned body, but still searching. I scarce know now how I got through the days, but in the evenings I would head straight for the village tavern and sit there drinking myself into a stupor, until Jeb, the landlord, would drag me to my feet and shove me out the door. I remember I wanted only to be by myself. I wanted no part of the talk that might be going round the room.

But one night I looked up and saw my friend Johnny Huntley, and it struck me strange of a sudden that he had spoken no word to me in all the nights I'd been there.

"Sit yourself down, Johnny lad," I said. "Have a glass with me."

"I'll drink with no wife-drownders," he answered short, and it fair knocked me cold. I sat stunned, not believing what I'd heard.

"How the hell do you mean me to take that?" I asked him.

"Take it as you've a mind," he answered. "It's what we all think, but only you know is it the truth or no."

"You're no friend of mine if you'd think that!" I rose to my feet and called to the landlord. "Jeb!" I shouted. "Drinks for all here, but none for this slanderous false rotten bastard who's no friend of mine!" And I emptied my pockets on the table.

"Nay," Jeb said. "You may drink here, for it's a public house I keep, but there's none here will drink with ye. So put away your money."

I turned then and looked at the faces of the men there. Friends they'd all been to me, or at the least neighbors, but there was no friendly sign from any of them. Some looked away, and some stared back at me like stone. It was plain they all thought as Johnny did, and a rage came over me that any of them could think I would have harmed Nora.

"May the lot of you drown in your own stinking bile," I shouted at them. "May the good drink turn to salt brine in your cups, and may you all die of thirst, for all I'll ever offer any of you drink again!" And damning the bloody-minded lot of them, I left that place and never went back again.

I did my drinking at home after that. My grief was so strong that it was only the drink that seemed to make my life bearable at all. But I'd have done better to drown my sorrow in a bucket of hog swill, for those evenings all ended the same, with Bab Magga comforting me, and her arms about me, and she in my bed, and me not wanting any part of her. Like the drink, she seemed to make my grief easier to bear, or so it was at first. Maybe the bitterness I felt toward my friends drove me to marry her, or maybe I had no choice at all in the matter. I'm certain now that it was her doing that the rumor spread that I had drowned Nora. If I had known it then, or even thought it, I'd have killed her rather than marry her.

But marry her I did. It was no proper church wedding, for Bab Magga would have none of that. We were married over the border where all that's needed is two witnesses, and not even a minister, to make it legal. For witnesses we had two old crones in black, cackling and drooling like crows over a bit of carrion.

It was a far different affair from my first wedding in the old Church of St. Inigoes in Fenwyck-Free. Ah! That had been beautiful! And when I put the ring on Nora's finger and kissed her, I knew then that I was the happiest man on God's green earth.

Miss Nora King she had been before we were wed, living with her widowed mother at Fenwyck-Free. It was eleven miles over the moors from our farm where I lived with my brother, Nat. We'd worked the farm together since our mum and dad died. Nat went for a soldier after I married, and now he's dead, and it's often I've missed him since. Not but what he was a sad trial to me when I was courting Nora. He could see I was serious in my intentions, and he was always trying to thrust a spoke in my wheel.

There was the night I was to take Nora to a dance, and I'd shined up the harness brass till it fairly outshone the sun. I dressed myself in my Sunday best, and I went out to where I'd left the bay mare harnessed to the gig. The bay mare was there, but the gig was gone. I cursed and yelled at Nat, for I knew he was somewhere about, laughing himself sick. I'd nothing else to use, for the farm cart reeked of dung, and the market wagon had two wheels off soaking in the pond. The hay wagon was there in the barn, still with a full load of hay. I was so desperate I even thought of unloading the hay and driving to the dance in that. But when I climbed up on the load with a pitchfork, there was the gig tucked away back behind the hay wagon in the barn. I had to harness the work team to move the hay wagon before I could get at the gig. I was raging so that I cursed every minute it took me, and I left the team and wagon standing there in the yard. When he saw me driving off in the gig at last, Nat came out laughing fit to be tied. If I hadn't been late already and eleven miles to drive, I'd have stopped and had a proper turn up with him. That's how it went. Every inch of my courting was like a hurdle race, what with Nat on one side and Bab Magga on the other. But it was worth it all to win Nora. She told me she'd never had a doubt from the minute I first asked her out.

We were married only two years when I lost her, and why I was ever fool enough to let Bab Magga into my house, let alone marry her, is what I could never understand, even while it was happening. It was no great bargain Bab Magga got, for my heart wasn't in it. More and more there was bitterness and open quarreling between us. There was no peace in our house night or day. And the worst of it was that I was no kind of father at all to my poor young son. Bab Magga saw to that. She twisted and turned us both about so that we fair hated the sight of each other. Ay, she'd always been clever that way.

The Son

OWEN

I was named Owen after my grandfather. He was lost at sea. I lost my mother too when I was just four days old, and my father married Bab Magga, the worst woman that ever lived.

It was because I was just a newborn babe that he brought her into the house, for he could not take care of me with my mother gone. It was Bab Magga alone who had the skill and the witchcraft to keep me alive. But there was no getting her out once she was there. It was her house after that.

They said in the village that my father had drowned my mother. But I knew that was a lie. My father never gave up grieving for her. In his cups, drinking strong whiskey, he and Bab Magga together, as they did night after night in the lamplit evenings, he would tell how he had lain under a spell and heard my mother leave the dark house—he, unable to rise —his limbs powerless to move—lying there hearing her go, as in a nightmare. When he could get up, he followed her. It was easy to see where she had passed, down through the wet meadow. He followed where the trail led down to the dark shore. Her footprints leading out across the sands to the water's edge. The tide coming in and no sign of her beyond that.

He called and shouted and waded out into the cold water almost to his shoulders and screamed her name, but he could not drown himself, as he was sure she must have done. What else was there to think? Only that she had walked out into the water and drowned. The reason for it he could not fathom.

"It was a spell on us both," he told Bab Magga.

And Bab Magga would say, "Ah, a sea demon's spell it was. And, oh the pity of it, that she didn't know the way to turn the spell. Now if it were to come about again, they would never bring *me* to the water's edge to draw *me* under. There's evil demons in the dark water, but they could never catch me, for I know how to guard against them. Ay, and I know how to turn the evil spell against those who would do me hurt!"

And she knew too how to hurt, how to bring a child to do wrong so she could punish him for it, and how to turn him into something he should never have been and gloat over him then for what he had become. She turned me into a creature full of fear and hatred. She even turned my own father against me, so that he hated the sight of me, and there was no one to help me.

I think Bab Magga must have been gentle with me when I was a small babe, for I remember none of the feelings of dread that I came to know later. Perhaps in those first years she was unsure of her hold over my father and so took care to treat me well. But as I grew old enough to walk and follow my father about the farm, I remember her hatred gathering about me, her punishments that I could not avoid even by trying to be good. Her laughter and her anger were both the same—both cruel. Her cruelties were small things at first. She would trick me into misbehaving and then punish me. And there were other things she did, like giving me vicious pinches under the table as we sat there eating, so that I burst out crying and my father would grow angry and send me away to bed without my supper. She struck fear in me with dreadful threats and told me the sea demons would come and steal me, as they had stolen my mother. This threat would throw me into a mindless terror, but finally there came a day when even the sea demons seemed easier to face than Bab Magga herself.

When I was little, she would take me with her to the cow barn every night to sit on a stool along the wall while she fed and milked the cows and raked out the dung. The barn cats fled when she entered, scrambling away and hiding in the dark shadows, their eyes glowing like green sparks in the lantern light. When my father was about the barn, the cats would come purring and rubbing against his legs. One old three-legged cat was especially friendly. My father told me she had been my mother's favorite. I remember one night in the cow barn while Bab Magga was in the hayloft, this old cat came rubbing against me and purring, so that I gathered her in my arms and buried my face and all my forlornness in her soft warm fur.

Then suddenly the cat was snatched out of my arms, scratching me as she was dragged away by her tail. I started up, crying out my protest, but Bab Magga was in a cold fury. I watched as she swung the screaming cat viciously against a beam. When Bab Magga flung the cat in the gutter, it lay limp and broken. I was terrified and sobbing loudly, but she began to laugh, and ordered me to sit down again on my stool.

"Sit there, you squealing shoat!" she whispered fiercely. "And if you cry, I'll do it to you too. I really will! I'll smash you to a bloody pulp!"

I sat stunned and sick, gulping down my tears, almost strangling on the sick terror that never quite left me after that.

Bab Magga kept me with her all the time, and I was always scared of her. I would rather have gone with my father, but she'd say, "Your father doesn't want you tagging after him. You remind him too much of your mother. He hates you for that." Whether it was true or not, that was what she would tell me, and so often that I came to believe it.

She always had chores for me, even when I was little. And when the chores were done, she'd take me with her gathering wild herbs and mushrooms and all kinds of grisly, grimly things—old smelly bones, and stinkhorns, and grubs and carrion beetles that she'd poke out of dead rotting carcasses. She would even poke out vipers from under rocks and catch them with a forked stick and toss them into a gunnysack. She would take these things home and cook them up in a big kettle, and the smell would choke a horse.

I felt sure my father had no use for me, but if he hated me, he hated Bab Magga, too. He got up early and came home late, working outside in the fields until long after dark. Perhaps he could not stand the smell of the house, though I remember only once that he said anything to her about it.

"When Nora was here this house was full of flowers," he'd said. "Now it stinks like death or worse."

Bab Magga had turned on him and yelled, "That Nora! To hear you tell it, she could dive head first into a muck heap and come up smelling all roses!"

My father had yelled back at her, and I thought he was going to hit her, but something seemed to check him, like a horse reined up sharp. Then Bab Magga started in laughing, and he just turned and slammed out of there. Most of the time he didn't talk to her at all, except when they were drinking together late in the night.

I was about five years old when I made up my mind to run away. I just got up one morning and I left. I didn't take anything with me. I just started walking. I didn't follow the road, I trudged up through the back pasture and through the wooded land and climbed the hill. When I looked down across the fields and glens and pastures on the other side, I saw the dark hills rising and the mountains beyond, violet color, all misty and faraway. I knew that was where I was going, and I felt as if I were journeying to the very end of the world.

I was hot and tired by the time I'd climbed the next hill, and I sat down among the flock of sheep that I found there and watched them. They were cropping sparse grass among the gray boulders of the hillside, and they paid me no mind. I was hungry and thirsty, but there was nothing to eat or drink. I wished I could eat grass like a sheep.

A flock of black birds flew over, and fear surged through me. Was one of them Bab Magga's jackdaw sent to spy me out? I got back on my feet and scrambled on down the hill, my legs working like pump handles, and the heart in me thumping like a fist against my ribs. I climbed stone walls and struggled through brush-filled gullies and trudged for miles. I found a fairy ring of mushrooms that I ate, and water in a brooklet, but I was footsore and dead weary and hard-set for my dinner when, in the late afternoon, I saw a farmhouse and outbuildings below me on the hillside. I felt a great joy, for I thought I had come at last to a safe place far away from Bab Magga.

The farm wife gave me a mug of milk and a meal cake, and I was so warm and trusting that like a noddycock I told them my name. The farmer saddled up a horse. "Come along, my lad," he said. "I'll be taking you home."

"No!" I screamed, backing away. "No! I don't want to go home!" and I started to cry.

"We'll just go for a ride then," he said, smiling, and I, poor little fool that I was, I smiled back up at him and knuckled away my tears. He set me up before him on the horse and off we went, and I enjoyed it rarely, sitting high on the saddle. We rode a long way through the dusky hills. I was nearly asleep when he pulled up the horse and spoke to someone. "Here's your wee little small lad," he said. "Running away he was."

I opened my eyes, and it was near dark. There was Bab Magga, like a bad dream, and we were in our own dooryard.

"I'll thank you for bringing the dear little one back," she said, all honey and sweet. "Ah no, he'd never run away. It must have been lost he was. He's the great one for wandering off."

I did not want to get down, but the man lifted me off the horse, and then Bab Magga was holding me tight by the arm, and the fear was in me so that I dared not cry out or protest. I knew her smiling talk was all false.

"You'll stay and have a drop of whiskey," she said.

"No, I'll not," he answered, rough. "Good night to ye." And he rode off the way he had come.

All I could think was that he had betrayed me to Bab Magga, and there was none in the whole world that I would trust ever again.

When he was gone into the darkness, Bab Magga turned on me. "You devil's spawn," she hissed, all poisonous again. "Run away, will you!" and she hit me a clout on the ear. "You've had your father and me wasting the whole day looking for you, and you not worth the candle to light you to hell! He's out there now, tramping the woods instead of doing his work as he should. Ah, you'll see what a whipping he'll give you when he gets back!"

My father had never whipped me, though he had yelled at me often enough. "He'll not whip me!" I cried. "He won't!" I was not at all sure that he wouldn't, for I knew it was a terrible thing I had done. But I defied her. "You can do it. I don't care. But I know he won't!"

That enraged her so that she grabbed me up in both arms and hustled me through the barnyard to the pigsties. She held me high over her head while I kicked and screamed. "Run away, will you!" she cried. "I'll see that you never run away again! I'll throw you to the sow and she'll eat your legs off. You'll not run far on the bloody stumps!"

The great brood sow was there below me in the pen, frothing and grunting as Bab Magga swung me through the air. The huge bulk of the beast with its long brockish snout loomed up toward me.

"What the devil are you up to, you black witch from hell!" It was my father's voice.

His coming was so unexpected that Bab Magga froze, still holding me high in the air. "The brat ran away," she panted. "But he'll not run away again!" And she flung me down into the foul, stinking mud of the sty.

The sow squealed and swung away, but then she turned and came at me, the great jaws champing, the long drools of spittle hanging from her chin. I shrieked and floundered in the muck, trying to get away from her. Then suddenly my father had vaulted over the fence and grabbed me up in his arms. I screamed even louder. I could feel the anger in his hands. But his anger was not for me. He was holding me, pressed tight against him, carrying me, kicking and struggling, toward the house. His rough bearded face was pressed against mine as he muttered terrible curses.

"Damn her!" he was saying. "Damn the foul witch! Damn her to hell! I'll kill her, lad. She'll not make your life a hell like mine.

"There now, lad, there now." He soothed me and hugged me to him. "She'll not harm you, lad. They say I drowned your mother. You know that's a lie. You know that, lad. I'd never have harmed Nora. But before God, I'll drown Bab Magga. Yes, by God, I will! Damned if I don't!"

He went on cursing her, but the curses sounded to me like love words. Slowly I realized I was safe, and my screams broke into sobs as I clung to him.

I remember his washing the muck off me, gently and lovingly, but I do not remember being put to bed or falling asleep. I know I slept, deep and heavy with exhaustion, and peaceful, knowing that my father's love was mine again like a warm thick blanket wrapped around me in the darkness.

But when I awoke, my father was gone and Bab Magga with him. As soon as I rubbed my eyes awake, I sensed that I was alone in the house, but I felt safe. I wondered at it a bit. He's taken her away, I thought, and I felt a fierce joy. I hoped he had taken her out to sea in his boat and drowned her. I knew they were both gone, but still I searched for him about the yard and outbuildings. Old Fadge, my father's collie bitch, followed me about, whining dismally.

I stayed away from the pigsties, though I could hear the hogs squealing shrilly for their breakfast. I took corn and fed the chickens and searched for eggs. I found a clutch of eggs under a blackberry bush and carried them warm into the house. There I took down the blue flowered bowl that I was forbidden ever to touch and broke the eggs into it, all of them, one by one. I took a loaf of new-baked bread and tore up bits of it to fill the bowl. I gave the rest of the loaf to

Old Fadge. Then I went down cellar to the milk shelf, where the rows of milk pans sat with the cream rising golden and thick to the top. I skimmed off a big dipperful of cream and poured this into my bowl of eggs and bread. I took down the jar of honey from the pantry shelf and dipped out the honey by spoonfuls. Then I sprinkled it all with two handfuls of dried currants and sat down to the table to eat.

I felt safe for the first time in many years. I ate slowly and savored each spoonful, and I enjoyed that breakfast as I had not enjoyed any other as far back as I could remember. And all the while I was thinking that my father had taken Bab Magga away to drown.

But as the day wore on and the sun got hotter, I began wondering when my father would return. Then I grew afraid again, thinking of the sea demons. Perhaps they had come to Bab Magga's rescue and pulled my poor father in his boat down into the black water. I began hoping he had taken her instead to Hangman's Hill and hanged her there, as I'd heard tell it was done. Or maybe he had built a great bonfire to burn her.

All day I thought about how she would die, many slow deaths, and all of them horrible, until at last the sun began dropping down in the sky to the west, casting long shadows over the yard and fields. I sat on the steps with the dog, feeling the day cooling off, watching the small gray-blue clouds light up one by one, their edges turning first pink, then fire-red glowing like embers. That would be all that was left of a witch after the burning. . . .

And then, looking down across the darkling meadow, I saw Bab Magga coming back, and my heart sank into darkness, back into its night of fear. She was coming back and dragging behind her on a chain a great brown goat.

Awakening

NORA

When I awoke in the castle—when I awoke from that dream of remembering—all I could do was weep. I hated tears. I had always hated tears. But it took a great effort to stop the weeping and force myself to think calmly. The babe had fallen asleep, and I laid him in his cradle, but myself, I did not dare to sleep. I was too fearful of losing my newfound memory.

I clung to my past as if clinging to my life, and as I sat there, gazing backward in time, the memories kept coming, tumbling out one on top of the other, all mixed up like a tangle of odd bits of yarn. All the small details of my life with Eben, the happy moments and the sad, the agony of childbed, and the joy in my new baby. I was tossed about in a great tumble of memories, reaching back all the way to my earliest years. I dwelled lovingly on each remembered scene:

helping my mother make scones in the sunlit kitchen of my childhood, breaking eggs into the blue flowered bowl of my married life, filling the warming pan with glowing coals on a black winter night, sweeping crisp autumn leaves across the stone floor of our farm kitchen. Each little thing that made up my life was examined and rejoiced over.

Memories of my father came back to me. A hearty black-bearded man in a captain's uniform. Almost a stranger to me when I was small, for he would be gone two and three years at a time, and not long home. But I remembered, too, my mother's grief when word came that his ship had gone down in a gale. Lost at sea! How we had dreaded those words. It was why I had early resolved to learn to swim. It was why my mother was so content that I had married a farmer, although she felt I was marrying beneath me. She had feared so that I would marry a sailor. Pictures flashed before my mind's eye: Sailors in striped jerseys danced a hornpipe under Chinese paper lanterns, all glowing rainbow-colored, strung from the ship's rigging. I saw my father standing on the deck of his tall ship the *Sarahnora,* named for both my mother and myself—one glorious night celebration of a successful voyage to the China seas. And the gifts my father had brought back from that voyage! Chinese dolls dressed in red and gold silk, a giant unfolding paper dragon, and jointed wooden tigers for me to play with. And for my mother, rolls of silk brocade, a Canton tea set, clay jars of ginger, and big square boxes of tea in flowered paper. China must be Fairyland, I had thought then.

Fairyland. Is this a castle in Fairyland, I wondered. A far different Fairyland from any I had ever imagined. But, thinking about this place where I was—this grim stone castle, now deep in darkness—I felt the strangeness, the foreignness, the otherworldliness of it. I rose then and lit all the candles that stood on the table and gazed about me, trying to discover where it was I might be. This was no English castle, nor like any I had ever seen in picture books. The furniture alone was so odd, so strangely carved, and the designs on the painted hanging cabinets were unlike any I had known. All seemed to be twining and twisting, turning and interweaving in intricate fantasy. On the table and chairs, grotesque carved faces peered out from amongst gnarled branches, and fabulous beasts chased each other over and under. I looked down at the garments I wore. They, too, were foreign, made of rich materials embroidered with strange designs. And the babe, sleeping in his cradle—the babe was no child of mine. That was the most terrifying thought of all, and again the tears caught me unawares.

The windows gradually grew lighter, and I rose to stare out into a limbo of gray fog where nothing was visible. I had seen many such foggy mornings, but now I felt as if the whole massive castle were unreal, floating in clouds, as if perhaps there were no real world outside at all.

The fish Clootie had flung at me was still lying on the stone floor, lifeless now and dull, all its bright color faded. I considered it; then, picking it up by the tail, I dropped it out the window. I heard it splash into the lake below. Somehow I felt reassured. There was a real world out there! If I strained to listen I could hear the faint mewing of sea gulls in the distance, and, outside the iron-studded door, I heard the tramp of feet, the voices of the guards.

Guards! I realized that now I could talk, I could speak to them! I tried the door. It was unlocked, and I opened it. I stared at the two men stationed there. I was aware for the first time of the strangeness of their garb, and the helmets! One shaped like a boar's head with ivory tusks, the other crowned with the antlers of a stag.

I drew a deep breath. "Where is Clootie?" I asked. "I must see him. Please tell him I desire to see him."

They stared back at me.

"She's talking," one said to the other.

"Yes, I hear her," the other answered.

"I must see Clootie! Right away. Right now!" I demanded.

"Who's she talking about?" Boar's Head said to Stag's Head.

"You can't expect to understand outlanders," Stag's Head said, staring right through me.

Were they half-witted? Of course they *must* understand. I realized with a slight shock that it was *their* language I was speaking, not my own.

"I must see Clootie," I repeated firmly. "Or the Erl Queen. I must see one or the other at once!"

The two stared at me, grim-jawed. "She's speaking of the *Queen!*" Boar's Head almost growled.

Even the guard dog growled at me. I looked down at the animal, directly into his eyes. His growling deepened, and he showed his teeth in a nasty snarl. Then of a sudden he let out a deep-throated roar and lunged at me. I slammed the door shut in sheer terror. What a monster! That dog had always ignored me before! I felt completely unnerved.

I sank down in a chair and stared out an eastern window into gray space. The jackdaw appeared in the window frame.

"Well-a-day," he piped. "Lack-a-day. Crack o' day! And when the sky began to crack, 'twas like a stick upon my back! Jack's back, Jack's back!"

"Dear Jack!" I said fondly, and noticed then, for the first time, that my gold ring was gone from my finger. "You wretched bird!" I cried. "You're still the thief you always were! Ah, but you did bring back my memories. I suppose I must thank you."

But suddenly a great black raven landed there on the sill beside him. Jack looked up at him in alarm and hunched his shoulders, sidling cautiously away. "Step on a crack! Break your back!" he muttered.

"Oh, go away, you ugly thing! Shoo!" I cried and waved my arms. But the raven remained; it was Jack who took off in fright.

"Carrrrrruck," croaked the big black bird. "And when the birds began to fly, 'twas like an earthquake in the sky!" His voice was deep and hoarse, as if muffled in woolen cloth, very different from Jack's shrillness, but clear as human speech.

His long throat feathers quivered. "You're a fool! I am the one you should thank. I am Munin. I am Memory!"

"Two talking birds," I exclaimed. "That's too much!"

"Too much!" the raven repeated. "Too, too much. Two too much." He clucked like a hen. "Two's company. Three's a crowd." And he turned, spread his wide black wings, and swept off into the grayness.

I jumped up and leaned out the window. But there was nothing there. Nothing at all.

"They're all the same!" I said aloud, impatiently. "They're all the same—talking birds! What they say sounds like sense, but it's nonsense. Where am I? Where *am* I? Am I nowhere?"

It seemed like nowhere. Nothing but fog, endless, fathomless, impenetrable. "Thick as pea soup," a sailor would have said. There *was* a greenish tinge to it! Slowly the garden began to emerge through the mist. The trees took shape first, as the sun glowed through the dense fog. I was relieved that the long night was over. I leaned on the windowsill watching the garden appear, first soft melting wet colors, then clearer and clearer. I could hear the small birds twittering and the water splashing in the fountain. It was a magical garden, with exotic trees and flowers such as I had never before seen. But now for the first time I could see its true differentness. And what meant more than all else, I could recall my homeland and my own past life.

The Erl Queen

NORA

The Queen's large silver-blue eyes fastened on me, and I felt the coolness of snow in that still gaze. I felt as if I stood in the center of endless silence. I stood in the rose-colored room, and where there had been warmth there was no warmth.

"Your Majesty," I said, "I have remembered whence I came and all that I left behind. I have come to ask your help in returning to my home."

I was about to continue, but the Queen interrupted me. "We know all that, Nora," she said. "We know all about you. But tell me, Nora, where is Hjuki?"

I was taken aback. If she knew all about me, why had she never told me who I was? Why had she not sent me home long ago?

"Come, Nora," the Queen said, and there was a hint of impatience in her cool voice. "Something has happened to Hjuki. Tell me, when did you see him last?"

It was Clootie she was asking about, although now she called him Hjuki. "When he threw the fish at me," I said. "Clootie flew into a wild rage, he threw the fish at me, I cried at him to stop, and then he vanished and my jackdaw flew in at the window. It was all very strange, and I still don't understand it."

The paleness seemed to increase in her face, the still quality to turn to a strange dismay. All the light in the room was gathered in her eyes, their silver shining brighter and brighter in the dark hollows. "Did you call him *Clootie?*" the Queen asked.

"Yes, of course I did. It was when he threw the fish at me."

"The fish is of no importance, Nora! But for you, an outlander, to call Clootie by his *true* name was a dreadful thing! It is my fault. I should never have revealed his true name to you, but how could I foresee that you would regain your speech? When you spoke Clootie's name, he was forced to change his shape. That would have been his only protection. *The jackdaw is Clootie.* But now he will have to remain a jackdaw until he renders you a service that none other can perform."

"The jackdaw cannot be Clootie!" I protested. "The jackdaw is from my other life. He was never anything but wicked and mischievous, and already he has stolen my gold wedding ring!"

There was a sharpness in her voice, the edge of a blade of ice, of moon-bright cold metal. "Never mind that, Nora!" the Queen said. "Promise me that whether he appears as man or bird, you will never call him *Clootie* again!"

"Very well, Your Majesty," I said. "I will promise never to call Clootie by that name again, but the jackdaw is from my old life. I know him well."

The tears started to my eyes as I thought of it, for with the jackdaw had come the dream and the memories. I tried to wipe my eyes. Why must I always give way to tears? But still my tears flowed, and there was no stopping them.

"Why are you weeping, Nora?" the Queen asked, and the coldness was softened, the ice melted to liquid as sweet as woodland water, a well of mysterious sorrow to share with me. "Is it for your gold ring that you weep? I will give you a whole purseful of gold for your nurse fee. You have taken good care of my baby. There is no need to cry, Nora. I value your service above all others. Please tell me what troubles you."

"It is for my own small babe I am weeping," I managed at last. "I left him when he was only four days old. What will have become of him with no mother to care for him? I know now how much he needs me, and I must go home!"

"You cannot go home yet, Nora!" the Queen said, and her words were like a sentence passed on me. "You must nurse the Erl Prince until he is strong enough to stand and walk alone, no matter if a dozen years should pass!"

I raised my head and looked full at the Queen, at the cold beauty, the river of silver hair—and those silver eyes! I understood now, for the first time, why I had been brought here. It was a terrible thing they had done, to take me from my own newborn baby and carry me off across the sea to this land where all was strange.

The knowledge angered me so deeply that my anger broke through my tears and I cried, "Why have you done this to me? Why could you not have found a nurse for your child here in your own land?"

The Queen's face grew stern as I spoke, but deep sadness was still in her voice, an overwhelming sadness. "All that matters to me is my child. I have powers to use, Nora, and I use them as I must. There was great need to bring you here, for I could not care for my own son. I have been ill ever since he was born, and even Raekkin can give me no healing. I had no milk for my baby. You were chosen, Nora, because you are a king's daughter, and only a king's daughter may nurse a royal babe of Erland."

"A king's daughter!" I cried. "You must know I am no such thing. My father was a sea captain. If it's a king's daughter you need, go find a king's daughter to care for your babe and let me go home!'

"Ah, Nora! You are of royal lineage though you may never have known it. You are of the direct line of King Owain, who ruled long ago in Strathclyde!"

I was speechless at this statement. Like the matter of the jackdaw, it seemed too fanciful to believe.

"I have tried to see that you are well treated, Nora," the Queen continued, and her voice was very weary now, like snow drifting softly through the room. Oh, the whiteness, the stillness, the emptiness of her voice! "You have no reason to weep. It were best to forget your past life. If you cannot put it out of your mind, we will have to try again to see that you forget. It is all Raekkin's fault for having dealings with Munin. If he had not come here, your memory would not have returned. *We will take care of it when Munin goes.*"

There was a finality in those last words that chilled me. Now I saw only frozen coldness in the Queen's pale face, and that cold went to my heart. To lose my memories would be a kind of dying. It was as if death stood between us and his hand might reach out and touch either one.

The Queen had been ill since first I had seen her, and this day she looked even paler, her skin almost translucent and the bones of the skull showing through. I knew that she was nearer death than I was, and the anger died in me, for I could not remain angry with one so frail and ill. But my voice was bitter as I spoke. "There is no need to rob me again of my memories. I love your child as dearly as ever I loved my own. I will nurse him gladly as I have done these many months, but I will hold you to your promise to let me go home once he is strong enough to stand and walk alone."

"Thank you, Nora," the Queen said, softly now, and it was like the sighing of leaves in a forest, feathery as swansdown brushing my cheek. "I shall hold you to your promise also. Take good care of my little son." Then she turned away and spoke to her handmaiden. "I am very weary now, and I must rest. But first we will give Nora a purse of gold from my treasure chest."

"I do not want your gold," I said. "If you would make me happier, then give me freedom to go where I will about the castle and let me walk in the garden, for I cannot bear being confined to one room."

The Queen did not answer for a long while. Her inner light was gone, her radiance, like snow afire, fading. Her skin seemed opaque now, like a milk-glass lamp unlit. She lay back, as if exhausted, with eyes closed. Finally she raised her hand and pressed it to her eyes. When she opened her eyes again, they seemed near blind, their silver sheen dimmed, tarnished and dull.

"Very well, Nora," she said. "It shall be as you ask, but the gold is still yours."

So it was that when I returned to the nursery it was with a page boy following, carrying a casket in which lay the bag of gold. But my heart was sick with the thought of the months that lay ahead, and as I gazed at the Erl child asleep in his cradle, a deep and terrible bitterness filled me.

The baby Prince stirred, trying to waken. He frowned and puckered up his face, clenching and unclenching his small hands. Then his blue eyes opened. He gazed up at me with a delighted smile, and the heart turned over in me.

I gathered him up in my arms and held him close. "Oh no," I whispered. "Indeed I love you, my poor sweet. Oh, I can't help but love you. You're Nana's darling, my only joy!"

It was true. I loved him. He was not my child, but I loved him, and he clung to me as if fearful I would leave him.

Heir to Magic

NORA

And so at last I was free to leave the nursery which I had come to think of as my prison, and I walked out into the magical garden. The trees were heavy-laden with fruit. Pears, apples, damsons, figs, and wineberries hung from the branches, lemons and oranges, too, and fruits I cannot name, all giving forth their fragrance so that the air was like spice. As I walked in the garden, I breathed in the sweetness of the air and listened to the small birds. The late flowers bloomed gold and purple. I carried the little Prince in my arms wherever I went. I was happy to see how much he enjoyed the flowers and the sunshine.

Clootie never did return, so the Queen sent Raekkin to take his place. I knew Raekkin only as the court physician, but he explained to me that he was not to be a steward as Clootie had been, but rather a tutor for the young Prince.

"Prince Elver will soon be a year old," he said. "It is time he learned Erlish wisdom and the things a prince must know."

I thought it must be because the Queen was as eager as I was to see her babe grown up, but how could so young a babe need a tutor?

Raekkin came often and spent much time with us. He did not set about trying to teach the baby Prince his letters or, indeed, instruct him in speech, but in a few months Prince Elver was prattling away at a great rate. He was still so frail and weak that he could barely sit up and crawl, but his mind was quick and far ahead of his body.

Raekkin did no more than play with the little Prince and talk to him as he showed him nursery games. In one game Raekkin would take off his coat and reverse it and put it on, waggling one arm in an empty sleeve and say, "See! I'm an elephant!" Raekkin would then take off Prince Elver's jacket and turn it inside out and show him the red lining. And he would say, "See! You put your coat on one way and it is one color. But if you *turn it inside out,* it is another color. Everything can be *turned inside out.* But unlike the jacket, not only the color will change but the form and even the nature of it. This is the most important lesson of all, for the first turning is very difficult, but there will always be new turnings."

And he showed the Prince a game very like cat's cradle that he called The Web of Seeming. Raekkin would say, "All things are like this web. You pick up two strings *so* and move them over and under *so*—and you have a new design! The changes are endless, though sometimes you will find that they repeat. Learning to control the changes is a long learning."

That was how Raekkin talked as he played with the babe. Prince Elver enjoyed the games, even if he could not understand the talk. How could he? I myself understood very little that Raekkin said.

I taught the babe the games I had learned when I was little: "Ride a Cock Horse" and "This Little Pig Went to Market" and "Sing a Song of Sixpence." The baby Prince enjoyed my games, but he was much more entranced by the games Raekkin played with him.

The jackdaw came and went. When he was about, he joined in the nursery games. He could play jackstraws as well as any human. Jack had always been a clever bird, but sometimes he was too mischievous to bear. I would be sitting knitting and look down to find that he had unwound my yarn ball and tied it in a botch of knots, or he would seize one corner of my kerchief and pull it off my head and go flapping about the room with it, squawking.

Everyone in the castle seemed to believe that the jackdaw was Clootie. Indeed, when I watched the bird, I could almost believe it myself. It was as if the bird had studied Clootie's mannerisms. But then I would remind myself that Jack had been my own household pet long before I had ever known Clootie. He was a part of my old life, and Clootie was no part of that.

"Jack's no thief! Jack's no thief!" the bird would cry when I scolded him.

I asked Raekkin to get me a cage so I could lock Jack up, but Raekkin glared at me and said, "Princess Nora, you've already locked him in a cage of black feathers. I'll not help you to lock him in any other sort of cage!"

Raekkin always called me Princess Nora. I did not like it, for others started doing the same and it made me feel foolish. When I protested, Raekkin said, "You can be a milkmaid or a mariner's daughter, if you like, in your own land, but this is Erland, and here you are a princess and a king's daughter, whether you like it or not!"

That was not the only disagreement I had with Raekkin.

Raekkin brought up the babe in his way, and I brought him up in mine, and we each tried not to get in the other's way. But sometimes we jostled against one another. As the months passed I kept trying to encourage Prince Elver to use his legs and stand, but his legs would go all rubbery, and he would start to scream as I held him up.

"Let him alone!" Raekkin said once, and his voice was harsh, almost angry. "Let him alone. He'll stand up when he is ready to. Many a man has stood up for a hundred years and never become a *man!*"

"But he must try," I insisted. "A baby has to learn by trying. He is old enough to walk."

And Raekkin snapped back at me. "Walking is not important in itself! If he were unable to walk, he could still be a man and a king and a warrior. There are worlds of mystery and magic that only the mind can conquer, but the battle is fiercer than ordinary men can face. When he needs to walk, he will walk. He does not *want* to walk now, because it would mean the loss of his mother."

"The loss of his mother!" I was astonished at such an idea. "How can his walking possibly harm Queen Elva?"

"It is not Queen Elva I mean," the little man said, and there was a strange look in his eye as he glared at me. "Queen Elva is very ill. The Prince's walking will not alter her condition. It is *you* he will lose if he learns to walk, and to him that would be as if his mother had died."

"How can you talk like that?" I cried. "I'm not his mother. I am only his nurse!"

"A mother is the one who loves and cares for us, not only the one who gives us birth!" Raekkin said.

Ah, that struck deep! "I know a child may feel that way," I said more quietly. "But how could the babe know what the Queen said to me about his learning to stand and walk alone?

How could so young a babe know that? Or understand what it meant?"

"What sort of child do you think you are raising?" Raekkin asked.

"Tell me then what sort of child he is!" I challenged him.

"He is Prince of Erland. He is Heir to Magic," Raekkin replied. His voice had a deep and resonant quality as he made this pronouncement. "Prince Elver understands far more than you realize. He knows not only the promise you made to his mother. He knows, too, your feelings about being forced to stay here."

I felt a wave of shock. Could the babe really know that I wanted to leave him? "What sort of magic is it?" I cried. "What sort of magic would make a babe understand my innermost thoughts?"

"That is not magic!" Raekkin said, and his voice was surly and gruff. "All children are far more *aware* than adults think. And this child is more aware than others!" And he would say no more to me.

I learned much from Raekkin, although I was often baffled by his manner of speech. For all his grouchiness, he was very patient. He taught me to read their writings—runes, he called them, and strange letters they were, like hen scratchings. But the books in which they were written were beautiful, the bright-colored, illuminated pages bordered with fantastic beasts and flowers. I loved turning the pages and poring over the intricately detailed pictures almost as much as I enjoyed the tales of enchantment that were recorded there. Strange and fanciful tales they were, of gods and giants and dwarfs, somewhat like the fairy tales I had heard as a child, but they seemed somehow more real here in this strange land.

I grew quite fond of Raekkin in spite of his odd manner. He was rough-spoken but gentle, and I came to trust him completely with the babe. Sometimes he would take the Princeling outside to play and allow me an hour or two alone to sew or read. Or I might leave him and the babe in the nursery and go out myself for a breath of air. I would climb the stairs to the tower top, and there I would lean on the stones of the parapet and gaze far out over the lake and forest to the marsh and beyond. On a clear day I might even catch a glint of the distant sea. High there on the tower top, I would reach out in my thoughts to talk to Eben. It was as if being alone there brought me closer to him. I would ask him how Owen was, and was the weather holding steady for the haying, were the new lambs thriving, and my hens still laying well.

"Ah, Eben," I would say. "Owen must be walking now. I'm sure he's sturdy and healthy! If you could but see the poor weak little thing that I'm nursing, you'd pity him. I am like the brocket cow that had the winter calf, poor rickety thing that it was. I remember its bones straightened out once it was out on grass. If grass could help my Princeling, I'd feed him grass! Perhaps it's my milk that's too thin, for he does not thrive as he should. They'd do better to find him another wet nurse, but they say only a king's daughter may nurse him. They believe I'm a king's daughter! They even call me Princess Nora. Ah, if you were here, Eben, we could laugh together over that! But oh, the years, the long years that are passing!"

Tears would come then to my eyes, but the wind would dry them where they ran crookedly down. Overhead the gulls and the ravens would be screaming, but I would not hear them, so rapt would I be with my thoughts of home.

If only the young Prince's body had been as strong as his mind, it would have eased my heart. But even when he was three years old, he was still barely able to crawl. I kept encouraging him to use his legs. I recall one day that he sat playing with a leather ball on the soft new green grass in the garden. When I told him he must fetch back his ball himself, he glowered so, his eyes so like the fierce eyes of an eagle, that the old lullaby came again to my mind, and I sang it to him there in the garden:

> Take time to thrive my ray of hope
> > In the garden of Dromore.
> Take time young eaglet till thy wings
> > Are feathered fit to soar.
> A little peace and then the world
> > Once more will have its due.
> Sing shusheen shurra lurra lay,
> Sing shusheen shurra loo.

"This isn't the garden of Dromore," he said firmly. "This is Castle Ellorgore. Where is Dromore?"

But I could not tell him, for it was only a song.

"You are a stupid Nana," he said. "You don't know anything. I'll ask Raekkin."

I knew I should scold him for that, but I had not the heart. He was so eager to learn, so full of questions, endless questions. "Why does the wind blow?" he would ask. Or, "What is the sky made of?" And his blue eyes would gaze at me, wide and profoundly thoughtful, as I tried to answer.

One day I told Prince Elver that his name, "Elver," meant "young eel," and he laughed at that.

"Call me Eel then, Nana!" he said.

"No, not eel, *young eel*. Or shall I call you Eelie? That means 'little eel' too."

He was delighted at the sound of it and repeated the name over and over, "Eelie! Eelie! Eelie!" until he was giggling and shouting it aloud with joy.

"Hush, Prince Elver," I said. "It is your secret name. I am the only one who will call you that, and only when we are alone."

"No, Nana," he said. "It is only my nickname. I will tell you my secret name, my *true* name, but you must never call me by *that* name unless maybe you need help, *real* help!" He looked at me with his blue eyes full of trust and big with his secret. "Because my *true* name is Hjälper, which means *Helper*, you know. A secret name gives you Power, but I don't mind if you have Power over me, because you are my Nana and I love you."

"Oh, Eelie, oh, my dear, dear little one!" I laughed with tears in my eyes and hugged him. For although I never quite understood this strange business of names, I did know that a *true* name was a very precious treasure here in Erland, and I was touched that my small Prince should tell me his.

And then one summer day when he was four years old, I sat on the stone rim beside the lily pool in the garden while Prince Elver balanced on his toes, his belly pressed against the rim of the pool, and leaned far over the edge, staring intently down into the pool. Deliberately he reached over to try to catch a bright fish as it swam past. I caught hold of him by the belt that circled his middle to keep him from falling in. He had often watched the fish, always with deep interest. I could see how strongly he desired to hold one, to examine the golden shining life of it. I laughed softly to myself as he leaned farther out, reaching toward the dark water, for I knew he would never be able to catch one of those swift darting bits of gold. I could not catch them myself, though I had tried to do so just to please him.

Suddenly he had dipped both hands in the water so quickly that my eye could not follow, and then he was holding up two fishes, one in each hand, holding them up gleefully for me to see. In each fist, tightly clenched, a golden fish squirmed.

"See, Nana!" he cried, his small face filled with delight.

"They are beautiful!" I gasped, completely amazed. "Oh, you are so clever! How did you catch them? I never could have! But let them go now, for they cannot live in the air."

"Yes, they can!" he cried. "Yes, they can!" and he opened his hands.

The two fishes did not fall back into the pool. As I watched, they swam out of his hands into the air, as if they were swimming through water. They darted about above the pool, two fishes of shining gold, flashing in the sunlight like small flames, like wingless birds, hovering above my small Prince's head.

I was speechless with the wonder of it. He giggled at my look of disbelief and dismay, for it was more than wonder. I felt; it was almost fright. Raekkin had told me he was Heir to Magic, but never before had I fully realized that he was moving so quickly into command of mysteries—mysteries I could not even begin to imagine—and still only a baby!

The Ravens of Odin

EELIE

My very earliest memory was of being alone with Raekkin on the top of one of the high towers, and there I emerged from darkness into light, like waking from sleep.

I remember the ravens and white gulls perched on the stones of the parapet as Raekkin stepped out of the door carrying me, a mere baby, in his arms. Most of the birds flew off when we approached, but two great black ravens remained. They spread their wide night-gleaming wings and bowed low.

"Greetings, Prince of Erland," they cried in their hoarse creaking voices. "Greetings, Heir to Magic and Mystery!"

They folded their wings again and looked at me with eyes like black shining beads.

"I am Hugin, I am Thought," said one.

"I am Munin, I am Memory," said the other.

"Prince Elver, these are my teachers," Raekkin said. He

set me on the merlon between them. "All that I know I have learned from them. They are messengers of Odin. They bring you the gifts of mind and memory."

I sat there, balanced on the square-topped stone, high above the world. I was too young to know fear, too young to understand how important this moment was. I reached out my hands and patted the smooth, shiny black feathers. "Nice birdies," I said.

"It is time to begin to *think*," Hugin croaked. "We will think together. Open your mind! Think as the winds blow, as the waves flow. Let the thoughts come clear, each thought a crystal drop of mind-dew. Feel the Power of thought flow through you. Feel the bright Power!"

My skin was all prickly, and I felt breathless. It was as if I could suddenly see a thousand things at once, as if light crackled and burned around me. I stretched out my arms wide to the wind and the clouds, and they seemed to sweep over me and engulf me. The waves of the lake below seemed to rush up to meet me. I leaned out, reaching toward the water, and would have fallen, but the two birds caught me and gently pulled me back.

"Do not go yet, Prince of Erland," I heard the muffled dark voice. "There is much to learn."

"To learn you must *remember!*" It was the voice of the other now. "Go back to the beginning. Remember the red sea in which you swam."

I remembered it. The warm salty water around me, the booming rhythmic heartbeat that I shared. The gentle rocking . . . back and forth, back and forth. Then a dreadful pressure, endless constricting pain, light blinding me, and a terrible lack of air. I scrunched up my eyes and shrieked! But the anguish ended. The air burned in my lungs as I gasped and gasped again. Then there was the long hunger, the gnawing empty feeling, the weakness that seemed to last for all eternity. And then the life-giving warm milk, the love, the comfort, the safety. But all at once the safety was gone. Fear filled me—*Nana wanted to leave me and go away!*

I opened my eyes and stared through tears at the bird. "Bad!" I whimpered. "You're a bad bird!"

His black wing brushed my face. "Forget then!" he said. "Close the door, but from now on you will hold the key to all your memories. Only your own hand will unlock the door!"

That was the beginning of my true life, a birth and a forgetting, and worlds and worlds opening before me, so many that I could not grasp them all. I could only catch glimpses of the endless procession of worlds twining and intertwining, forming patterns and breaking away again to form new patterns. Raekkin was there to guide me safely and carefully step by step, and Nana was there to enfold me in her warmth and love.

I asked Raekkin questions, and he gave me careful and complex answers that I had to puzzle over and untie bit by bit like complicated knots. I asked Nana questions and she gave me simple, silly answers. She thought I was still a mindless baby.

I remember when I was three years old asking her, "What is the sky made of?" And she said, "It's made of so many things, Eelie, my love. There's the moon that's made of green cheese, and the cow that jumps over the moon. The cow makes the Milky Way. And then there's the cat that plays on a fiddle to make the wind howl, and the old woman who shakes her featherbed so that the snow flies."

It all sounded so funny to me that I couldn't keep from laughing. "Oh, Nana!" I said. "You know that's all baby nonsense. You mix things up. Don't you *know* what the sky is made of?"

"What do you think it's made of, Eelie, my pet?" she asked.

I had given it a great deal of thought, for the sky was different from everything else. There was nothing there, but it was not empty. There were wind and clouds, and you could feel the air, but you couldn't see it.

"It might be something like blue glass," I said doubtfully. "Or maybe it's more like dry water. Birds fly in the air just as fish swim in the water. If I had wings, I'd like to fly there, too."

"If you are good, you will grow angel wings," Nana said, still humoring me. She would not take my thinking seriously. "Let me see if you are growing wings yet." And she ran her hands over my shoulder blades. "I can almost feel the wings growing," she said. "But you will have to eat your porridge without fussing before you can grow angel wings."

I was impatient with that sort of talk. "I will *not* grow angel wings," I said decidedly. "I will grow eagle wings! You sang about my growing eagle wings."

Nana nodded. "You are my eaglet and my dove and my angel—but I would rather have you walk than fly. You know you could walk, Eelie, if you would only try."

I did try. I kept trying, but I could not even stand up by myself. Why did I have to keep on trying to do the impossible? Why did Nana still want to go back to Owen, her lost baby? She did not even know Owen. He can't love her anywhere near as much as I do, I thought.

"I can *not* walk," I said. "Someday I will fly, but I will *never* walk! You just want to go away and leave me!"

"Oh, Eelie!" Nana cried guiltily; she was very upset. "Oh, Eelie, it isn't that. I just want you to grow healthy and strong."

Why did she try to fool me? I knew how she felt.

Thinking about the difference between sky and water made

me curious about fishes. I studied the goldfish in the lily pond in the garden. Beneath the green lily pads and white water-lily flowers, deep in the murky depths, the bright golden fishes darted in and out of the shadows, glinting briefly as they passed through the beams of sunlight that shone down through the water. I concentrated on them with intense interest until one day I reached into the pool and caught two fishes in my hands. When I let them go again, they swam about in the air. They were even brighter, even prettier than birds, all shimmering and sparkling like real gold.

But Nana was disturbed and unhappy. She knew it was magic. It was nice magic, but she was afraid of things she didn't understand. At that time, I couldn't see why anyone would feel that way. There were so many things I didn't understand, endless things, but I wasn't afraid of them. Even when I was really little, I wanted to learn about everything. Raekkin had showed me how to *turn things inside out*, to take them apart and put them together in new ways. That was what I had done with the fishes.

I was so young then, so innocent. The unknown should always be treated with deep respect, but then, at that time, I thought it was all a beautiful game. I knew how everything could be controlled, if only you understood it, but I had yet to realize how difficult it was to achieve that control, and how dangerous.

PART TWO

The Spells of Erland

The Goat

OWEN

I watched Bab Magga coming up through the darkling meadow, leading the big brown goat. A despair and a dread swept through me, and then I was running down the meadow toward her. "Where's my dad? Where's my dad?" I screamed at her. Old Fadge barked at her.

She just laughed at me.

"He'll never come back again," she said. "You'll not see him again!" She could see my dismay and fear, and she gloated over it. "He tried to get the better of me. He turned on me—that's what he did! But no one gets the better of Bab Magga. Just you remember that! I know how to deal with anyone who turns against me."

In the morning I screwed up my courage again and asked, "Where's my dad? What did you do to him?" I was terrified that he was dead, but still I asked.

"Do you really want to know? Do you really? Well, I'll tell you! I changed him into a goat, into that big brown goat. And now he's tied up on the hill back of the barn, and he'll stay there! And if ever you run away again, I'll turn you into a pig, I will!"

I believed her at first and wept secretly for my lost father. For a long time after, I thought of the goat as my father and felt a deep love for him. But as I grew older, bit by bit I stopped believing and decided the goat was just a goat.

Bab Magga and I lived alone on the farm after that. She sold Old Fadge, and she sold the cows, all but one. She kept one cow that was an easy milker. Moorland Meg was her name, and Bab Magga taught me to milk her. There was a lot of hard drinking she did, and when she got drunk she'd throw things at me. But it was not the drink that was the worst. There were other things she did—real gruesome spookish witchcraft—that scare me even to think about.

In the spring Bab Magga planted no crops, just the few vegetables for our own use. I learned to hoe and pull weeds when I was still only half as high as the hoe handle; by the time I was nine, I was doing all the work in the garden as well as the chores about the place.

Bab Magga had me, too, gathering the wild herbs and catching the snakes and toads and salamanders she needed. She'd send me up on a ladder high into the barn peak to pluck bats off the rafters, where they hung like ripe plums for the picking. I wasn't scared to climb way up high, and I wasn't scared of the snakes or bats. It was only Bab Magga I was scared of. Some of these creatures she kept alive in cages, but not as pets. They were for making spells. Some she killed and hung from hooks in the kitchen ceiling to dry. There was always a dead rotting smell about the house, but I got so I didn't notice it.

Nobody from the village ever came in our house. They all knew Bab Magga was a witch, and they were scared even to knock on the door. If they wanted her to do something for them, to cast a spell or the like, they'd come and stand in the yard and yell until she came out. They treated me, too, as if I were some sort of witch child. I could see that they looked at me with horror and disgust, and it made me feel there was something loathsome and foul about me.

That was why I liked the brown goat. He smelled bad and he was as much an outcast as I was. He was kept tied up and alone on a rocky hillside. I felt that the goat and I were alike. I would sit beside him in the nest of bent bracken where he lay and stare into his eye—into his golden eye where the pupil floated like a black bean.

His horns sprang up black and shiny with ridges ringing them, deeper than the ridges in a cow's horns by which you tell her age. When I ran my hands over the rough curve of his horns, the goat would arch his neck and lower his head, hoping I would scratch behind his horns. Bab Magga called him Eben, but that was my father's name. I felt she called him that out of spite and to make me keep thinking that he was my father. But I could not think of him that way any more, for when I talked to him, as I often did, there was no flicker of understanding in his eyes. They were goat's eyes, golden and expressionless. If he was my father, as Bab Magga said, why did he give no sign? He must have forgotten all about being a man. He would lie there chewing his cud and flicking his ears at the flies that buzzed about him. I felt a love for the goat, but I could not call him Eben. I tried to think of a name for him, but I could not think with his honey-gold eye so close to mine.

One day when I was nine years old, it happened that I was sitting there with the goat, running my hands through his brown shaggy hair, stroking his neck. His beard was tangled and knotted. Absent-mindedly I began to work on one of the knots, picking at it slowly and patiently until at last the knot was loosened and the hair combed out smooth between my fingers. The great goat got up and shook himself. He rose in the air, cavorting on his hind legs. He was so big, as big as a pony! I jumped up and away from him, for it was as if he had suddenly become a different and dangerous creature.

He dropped his forelegs to the ground, lowered his head and charged—not at me, but straight ahead the full length of his chain. I thought the chain would break. I wanted it to break. I wanted him to be free. But the chain held, and in the end he was brought to his knees with the breath choked from him, as he struck the end and crashed against an invisible wall. He rose, dazed, shaking his great horned head, and then he raced full speed once around the full circle of his tether. I turned and ran back to the house.

That night as I slept, dog-tired as always, I heard voices. One voice sounded like the voice of my father. I wanted to wake up, to call out to him, but I could not. It was like a dream sleep, but not the same. I was only half awake at best.

Bab Magga's voice said, "Who untied it! Who dared untie the first of my seven knots?" Her voice became soft and coaxing, and that was more frightening than the menace in her first question. "Tell me, my pretty honey one. Tell me, my dearie."

"You can go to the devil!" my father's voice answered her.

"Ah, yes. We'll be going there together, my sweet pet. This is the sabbath night, the Black Sabbath, dear heart. You'll be carrying me to the devil tonight, whether you like it or not."

"I'll carry you to hell gladly and leave you there, if they'll have you. Even the devil himself would have his fill of you soon enough!"

"You've a bitter tongue in you tonight. It's that knot being undone. Now tell me, my pet, who did it? Who was it untied that knot?"

My father's voice replied, "It was the jackdaw did it."

"If it was him, I'll pluck out his feathers and roast him on a spit; and though he'll be tough eating, I'll eat him!"

"You can eat him raw or roasted," said my father's voice. "I don't give a damn what you two do between you."

"He was always a jackanapes and not to be trusted. He takes too many liberties," said Bab Magga. "I need no jesters in my company. A black sending it was, the day he was chosen to be the go-between. But hold quiet now, my pretty, and I'll tie the knot back again as tight as tight.

> *"Tight as tight*
> *Neat as neat*
> *And the spell*
> *Will be complete.*
> *Wind and twist*
> *Turn and twine*
> *Over and under*
> *To keep you mine."*

The singsong chant of her voice numbed my mind, and I heard nothing more, for sleep overcame me.

Witch Knots

OWEN

The next morning when I came in from milking the cow, I found Bab Magga making ready to leave the house. She'd had word that Katie Hannah was "in difficulties." That meant she was slow having her baby. They had to be desperate to send for Bab Magga, but they always turned to her and her witchcraft if babies weren't coming right, or if they wanted her to put a curse on a neighbor. Bab Magga was happiest making curses; she didn't much care about bringing babies into the world, except that sometimes it would turn out to be a monster with legs coming out of its shoulders or two backsides joined together and no head. She was always excited about monsters and tried to keep them alive. But I don't think any of them ever lived. She was a lot more skillful than the midwives; if the baby was slow coming, they sent for Bab Magga.

"Hoe the turnips and pick the worms off the cabbages. Pick the bugs off the potatoes and hill them," Bab Magga said, listing all the things I was to do while she was gone. There was a lot more on the list, and all the regular chores, too, but I didn't need reminding about them. Milking the cow, slopping the pigs, feeding the hens, hauling water from the spring, bringing in wood—those were the things I did every day anyway.

She wanted to be sure I'd have things to do every minute she was away. She told me she might not get back before evening. She took the smallest black pig with her and a black cockerel in a basket. The jackdaw had flown off, or she would have taken him. He helped her work spells; the other black animals were second-best. She went off down the road in the horse-drawn wagon. I watched her getting smaller and smaller. I wished she really were getting smaller and would shrink away to a small black bug that I could step on. But I was glad to be free for a day. At least I *felt* free once she was gone, even if she had left me all the work to do.

I did the things she had told me to, but I skipped picking the worms and the bugs. There would be more worms and bugs tomorrow, even if I picked them, so she would never know if I had done it or not. I'd been thinking about the goat all the time I was hoeing the garden. When I had finally finished hilling the potatoes, I put down my hoe and ran up through the pasture to the rocky patch where the brown goat was tied.

He came toward me slowly and lowered his head, bobbing it up and down—in greeting, so it seemed, but I knew he just wanted me to scratch behind his horns. It was the one place he couldn't reach. He stood stock-still, his eyes golden and empty, as I scratched his head. He would stand there for as long as I scratched him.

But I wanted to examine the knots in his beard. I knew there was some secret about those knots, and I wanted to discover what it was. I was excited remembering my father's voice, knowing that he was still alive and that he had come back the night before—even if he hadn't come into my room to see me. I knew it was not just a dream. There was some secret that he knew about the goat.

I started talking to the goat, as if I were talking to myself. It was good to be talking to somebody—even a goat—even if he couldn't understand a word.

"There's something about those knots in your beard, Goat," I told him. "Something Bab Magga doesn't want anyone to know. Hold still now and let me look at them. They look like knots you'd get from burrs tangling up the hair, but they're really tricky. Bab Magga made them on purpose. And there are seven of them. Just as she said. Seven knots. Let me work on one of them. Now just hold still. Just think about how nice it would be to find out Bab Magga's secret. Do you think she's hidden something inside the knots?"

The goat held still, his eyes expressionless and golden, while I sat beside him in the brush and worked at untying the knots.

"My father is alive," I told him. "He came back last night, and I heard him talking to Bab Magga. I'm glad the sea demons didn't drown him. I wish he would come and take me away. If he knew she wasn't here today, he might come and get me. I wish there was some way to tell him. I don't think he's afraid of her, as I am. Everybody else is afraid of her. But you know that. If everybody wasn't afraid of her, I would run away. But I know they would help her catch me and bring me back. I wish there was some place I could go, where she couldn't ever get me!"

I finished untying the first knot. There was nothing in it that I could see, but I went on talking like that to the goat and working on the knots as I talked. After a while, as it got late, I just let my fingers work and kept my eyes on the road. I could see it from where I sat, and I kept watch so I could run back down to the garden if I saw Bab Magga coming in the wagon.

But the sun started going down, and I'd only finished untying four knots. I knew I had to get back·to the house and do the evening chores, because if Bab Magga came home after dark, she'd punish me if the chores weren't done. So I left the goat and ran home and did all the things I was supposed to do. I even did the things Bab Magga usually did, like pouring the milk into pans and carrying it down cellar. When it got really dark and Bab Magga still had not come home, I ate some cold boiled potatoes she'd left in the pantry. I knew she might come back any time, so I didn't do anything I wasn't supposed to. I wanted to slice off some cheese and ham, but I didn't dare. I just ate the potatoes and went to bed. It was bad enough to have fooled around with the goat, I didn't want her to have anything else on me. If she came back late, she wouldn't look at the goat. Sometimes she didn't look at him for a day or two. I hoped she wouldn't. I really wished she'd stay away two or three days. Sometimes she did.

Maybe wishing helps, though I have never been sure it does. But in the morning she still had not returned home. Somehow, I felt it was my last chance to get those knots out. I was almost frantic, I was so anxious to do it. It was as if I were obsessed. As soon as I woke up and found I was still alone in the house, I ran right out and up the hillside through the wet grass to where the goat waited. I kept watching the road, and I kept working on the knots. It was as if I were in a fever. I had brought my knife, but I didn't dare to cut off the beard hairs with the knots in them, because then Bab Magga would know for certain that I had done it.

The morning got hot and flies began buzzing around. The goat lay there quietly, chewing his cud, his eyes golden and unseeing, as if he were far away, thinking of other things.

Goat Thoughts

EBEN

Bab Magga did me a favor when she turned me into a goat.
For one thing, I was free of any desire I'd ever had for her.
For another, I was free of the urge to strong drink, which was
near to mastering me. Whenever I'd thought of what my
life had become since I'd lost Nora, it had been only the drink
that could bring me to accept it and go on living.

Now there I was, a goat lying in the crushed bracken, a
prisoner chained to a stake, and the devil alone knowing what
Bab Magga would want of me when that mad witchcraft of
hers led her into deeper and fouler dealings with demons and
such.

I felt strangely at peace being a goat, if she would but leave
me alone. I was happiest when my small son came and talked
to me, but it was as if he were far away and in another world
and I in a world where all that mattered was the taste o

leaves, and a bellyful of them, and the warm feel of the sun that was a comfort, or the buzzing and biting of flies that were an annoyance. I lived in a goat's world, and my son, still in the world of men, talked to me about things that did not matter any more.

He sat beside me working on the witch's knots that Bab Magga had tied in my beard. I knew they were all that kept me from breaking my chain, but I had small hope that Owen could untie all seven knots and win me my freedom. He did not know what it was that he was doing, but he would do anything to spite Bab Magga. He still led a miserable life, poor lad, as we both had—hating each other for no reason but that Bab Magga made it happen so.

But if I thought of these things as I lay there in the bracken, it was not like a man thinking. It was a different sort of thought—like a goat's. But I know I was remembering more and more of what it was to be a man, as Owen worked on those witch knots and talked to me all the while. He had climbed up and straddled my shoulders, and his arms were around my neck as his fingers worked on the knots. It was strange how I began to feel more and more eager and restless as the knots came undone one by one. But I lay quiet; I was not going to spoil it this time, as I had before, by trying too soon.

When the last knot fell apart, I rose to my feet smoothly, so as not to unseat Owen. He clung there, his arms clasped tight about my neck, and I ran. I ran seven times around the circle, with Owen laughing aloud, and then I charged full force against the full length of the chain of spells. The three hundred separate links of it shattered and flew scatterwise like bird shot—and I was free!

I was free, but I was only partly free, for I was still a goat and not a man. It was a bitter blow to find myself still in goat's form. Some essential part of the spell was still unbroken. But I knew this was my one chance to get away, far away, from Bab Magga. That was why, when the chain parted, I never stopped running. I went galloping off across the hill fields with Owen yelling at me to "Whoa!" But he was too delighted to be really frightened, and he held tight to my great curved horns as I raced through the woods and down to the shore. I galloped along the rocky shore, and my goat's hoofs never slipped as I leaped from rock to rock.

At first I had no thought of where I was going—my sole thought was to escape from Bab Magga. That was enough. Then, as I ran, I began to remember clearly a place, an island, where my mother had taken me when I was a boy. Rowan Tree Island it was called, because of the rowan trees that grew there. We had rowed out to it in the autumn to pick rowan berries that my mother would make into marmalade. She had told me then, long ago, that where rowan wood grew, witches had no power. Now, as I thought of that, I knew where to go. I had to take Owen there. Perhaps on that island I would become a man again.

I turned toward the sea. I galloped down the rocks and plunged into the water, not thinking about the fact that I had never swum before, not doubting that I could swim. And I swam. Away out in the bay I could see the islands scattered. I did not know if I could swim that far, but I knew that I must. For myself, I had no fear of drowning, but Owen, poor lad, was terrified. His legs were clamped tight around my middle, and his hands clenched to my horns. I was glad it was not my neck he clung to, for I would scarce have been able to breathe, and I needed all the breath that was in me and all my strength. As I swam farther and farther out, Owen railed and cursed at me and ended by weeping in terror.

The icy water sapped my strength, but I swam steadily. My determination was such that it filled my whole being. The choppy waves slapped hard at my face; the morning light on the water dazzled and half blinded me, but I kept my eyes fixed on the one island. It lay there far away, drawing me to it. I fought to reach it. I fought against weariness and hopelessness and despair. Slowly the island drew nearer, grew larger, until we came, at last, into the shallows where my hoofs touched bottom, and Owen slid from my back.

I staggered up the rocky beach. There ahead of me I saw the great rowan trees standing. I felt a great surge of hope as I reached the nearest one. I leaned against it, my heart thundering in me, my sides heaving as I drew in long desperate breaths. In my goat's mind I prayed a prayer—half human, half animal—a plea to be restored to my manhood.

Overhead I heard the voices of the great trees murmuring —deep and majestic those voices, flowing into my heart:

> *We are the Rowanwood.*
> *We are the haven,*
> *The place of safety from evil powers.*
> *We offer you peace.*

"*Help me,*" I pleaded deep in my soul. "*Make me a man again!*"

"*We are the haven,*" the trees answered:

> *We cannot restore you.*
> *We cannot undo the spells of Erland.*
> *We can only cleanse you of evil*
> *And preserve you in safety.*
> *We can protect you and comfort you.*
> *We are the haven.*

Then my head drooped in my deep discouragement and

despair, my strength gave way, my goat legs crumpled under me, and I lay there with my eyes closed. The warm sour cud rose in my throat, into my mouth. The soothing juices flowed as I slowly chewed it. I lay there, my mind sliding wearily into a drowsy peace, back into animal contentment. My small son sat beside me. I felt his arms clasped around my neck. I heard his voice, but his words had no meaning for me. All I heeded were the gentle voices of the rowans rustling, murmuring:

Haven . . . Safety . . . Peace.

The Erl King

∽

EELIE

I remember music floating through the garden, sweet and tinkling, like bells under water. I was just three years old then, and Nana was carrying me down the path where the orange and lemon trees grew in big tubs. The golden fruit glowed among dark shiny leaves. We came to where the King was sitting on a bench with three young and very pretty ladies of the court. One was playing a lute and one a lyre.

Nana was about to go another way, but my father called her over to him, calling her "Princess Nora," and told her that he wanted to look at me. I could tell he wasn't pleased with me even before he spoke.

"So this is my son," he said loudly in a great booming voice like a drum. "Phah! What a miserable brat, still as puny as ever. Don't you feed him? He's as scrawny as a mongrel pup. If he wasn't my only legitimate offspring, I swear I'd disown him!"

I did not say a word. I looked up at my father and wondered at his showing such open contempt for me. Was he
trying to shame me into changing? I was at least fair of face,
and he was so gross, so big and ugly, all warty and repulsive.
How could *he* scorn me?

But Nana was flushed and upset. She didn't know what
to say. The King seemed to notice her then, and it was as
if he forgot me completely. He looked hard at Nana in
such a strange way and laughed then and told her to put me
down on the grass and come sit beside him. She did this,
and he held her hand and stroked it. I knew he thought
Nana beautiful, with her serious face and her dark hair and
eyes, but I could sense the way he felt about her, and I
didn't like it. I knew he admired her, but he was also pleased
that she shuddered when he touched her. He was so ugly in
her eyes! And he knew it and liked her to feel disgust and
loathing for him.

I knew he could have made himself handsome if he had
wanted to. I was sure he could do that. Raekkin had told
me that we are not all Shape Changers in this land, but I
knew I was one, and so were my father and my mother. But
my father didn't want to be handsome. He wanted to be
ugly, and the other ladies did not mind his ugliness. I
could feel that they were all drawn to him, to his ugliness. It
was almost as if his ugliness were what fascinated them.

He turned to one of the ladies, a fair-haired one dressed in
green with rubies in her hair. "Sing us 'The River of Flowers,'" he commanded. She bent her fair head over her lute
as she struck the first rippling chords of music. Then she
lifted her head and smiled at him and sang:

> *I sing of a river, the River of Flowers,*
> *With water as sweet as nectar.*
> *Through the King's wide bed*

The River of Flowers runs,
And all the white horses of the King
Come to that river to drink
The waters as sweet as nectar.
Never was such a sweet river;
Nay, never another so fair flowing.
Never were such fair white horses
As the horses of the King.

The song told me everything. I knew that they were lovers, my father and that lady. I knew, too, that he had many lovers, many fair women. For the first time in my life I felt hatred. I hated him for wanting Nana too. I knew what it was that he felt toward her, a craving for her, a craving to hurt and destroy her. I thought of my mother, the Erl Queen, pale and sick, and I felt such rage swelling within me that I could hardly hold it inside myself.

My father must have felt my anger, for he turned to look at me. I sat there on the grass before him, glaring up at him, and he glared back at me, a huge monstrous troll. He seemed to grow larger and larger, and I felt myself shrinking. I knew he was trying to force me to change into something even smaller than I was, into something like a small insect that he could crush. He turned such malevolent Power on me that I could not keep from crying. Suddenly I was only a weak baby, red-faced and screaming, squalling my lungs out in a red blur of terror and rage.

I felt Nana snatch me up and try to comfort me, but I could not stop shrieking—my whole body was racked with fury. I heard my father's voice booming out, "Take the damn brat away!" and as I was carried off, still howling, I heard him laugh.

I must have cried myself to sleep like a baby, and I remember that when I woke up in Nana's lap back in the nursery, I still felt like a baby, but I was happy again. I loved Nana so much. She smelled milky sweet and warm like toasted buns and so comforting! She rocked me in her arms and sang to me, one of her silly baby songs about the Queen in the parlor eating bread and honey. I knew the bad part was coming—about the blackbird snapping off the nose—and I didn't want to hear it.

So I said, "I'm hungry, Nana!"

But then she reached out and took an orange from the bowl and started to peel it, and it got all horrible again inside me. The orange smell tingled in my nose and brought back the scene in the garden and the terrible hatefulness. I still could feel the overwhelming Power that my father had turned against me. It was dark purple-red and dreadful.

"I don't want the orange!" I screamed at Nana and pushed it away. "I hate oranges. I wish Raekkin was my father. I like Raekkin, he's a good man. My father, the King, is not a good man. He's *bad*. I don't want him for my father!"

"Oh, Eelie," Nana said gently. "You can't just change fathers whenever you want to."

"Why can't I? He hates me and I hate him!"

"He doesn't hate you, Eelie. It's just that he's the King, and he doesn't have time for you the way Raekkin does. It's very important work a king must do. He has to rule over the whole land of Erland and take care of it. He just doesn't have time to play with you."

"He has time to play with those ladies!" I said.

For some reason that upset Nana. I could tell. She got red in the face and didn't answer.

I was beginning to feel more like myself again. "I wish you'd marry Raekkin," I said. "Then you could be just like my father and mother, even if you weren't really. It wouldn't matter about the Erl King and the Queen. We could pretend they weren't here. We could forget about them."

Nana smiled at that. "I do like Raekkin, Eelie, though we have our disagreements. But you know I'm married already. I can't marry again, and I wouldn't want to marry anyone else, because I love Eben, my husband."

"What is Eben like?" I asked.

"He's tall and he has broad shoulders and brown hair and a beard, and he's a farmer, and he's a good man, hard-working but always full of fun. We were so happy together, he and I. And when Owen, my baby, was born, it was the happiest time of all."

"Didn't Eben hate Owen?" I asked.

Nana was shocked. "Eben hate Owen! Oh, no! Eben was so proud to have a son. He was so good, so kind; he was so careful with young things—young plants and animals— I'm sure he's taking good care of Owen. Oh, Eelie, that's the only hope I have left. I know Eben will care for Owen until I get home. It was cruel to take me away from them. . . ." Nana's voice got all broken up.

I was sorry I'd stirred up her feelings so much. She always got like that when she thought about her home and Owen, the baby she'd had to leave behind.

I put my arms around her neck tight and said, "Don't worry, Nana, you've got me. I'll never let anyone take you away from me ever!"

The Island

OWEN

When the goat broke free and started running off with me on his back, at first I was frightened. Then I began to feel excited and glad to have him carrying me off. But when he plunged down the shore and into the water, I started yelling, "Whoa!" again. He didn't stop, and I screamed curses at him and begged him to take me back. We were out in the water before I realized what was happening, and then I was really afraid. Suddenly I began to think he was carrying me off to the sea demons, that this was all Bab Magga's doing and my punishment for untying those knots. The fear was so strong that not only the teeth shook in my head, but I shook all over. My hands were clenched tight on the goat's horns. I did not dare let go. Only his head was out of the water as he swam steadily farther and farther.

By the time we were out in the middle of the bay, I was

ready to give up and accept drowning. Maybe it wouldn't be so bad an end. My life had been a misery for as long as I could remember. By the time I realized that the goat was heading for one of the islands far out in the bay, I was even ready to let the sea demons take me. But as we came closer to the island, I began to have hope again and think that maybe the goat was carrying me to safety.

That island was beautiful to see. When we came into shallow water, I slid off his back and waded ashore after him. He walked slowly up the beach to the edge of the woods and stopped under a big rowan tree. He leaned against the tree and stared around with glassy eyes. His ears swiveled as if he were listening to something. Then his head drooped and he stood there looking like a horse that has run too far and too hard. He just hung his head as if it were all over with him, and then his legs folded under him and his eyes closed.

I was afraid he was going to die. I knelt down by him there and put my arms around his neck and talked to him. "Don't die, Goat," I said. "You'll be all right. I'll take care of you, Goat. I'm glad you brought me here. I would rather stay here and starve than stay with Bab Magga, but you mustn't leave me all alone!"

I pressed my face against the wet hair of his neck and I wept. Then after a while the gold eyes opened, and he started chewing his cud with a sort of dreamy look. So I knew it was going to be all right with him.

If I had known I was going to run away with the goat like that, there are a lot of things I might have taken with me. But I had not planned on running away, so all I had were the clothes I was wearing and my knife. If I had not had the knife, I don't think I would have lasted long on the island alone with the goat.

I was ready to starve, but I kept finding things to eat. Day by day I got used to looking for my food, climbing over the island and visiting the berry patches each morning, looking for mushrooms, picking wild greens to eat. I knew all the wild plants, and I knew which mushrooms were good to eat. Those were things Bab Magga had taught me, though usually it was the poisonous sorts she had sent me out to find. I ate anything I could catch, even frogs and snails. I never got so I could hit a bird with a stone, but I raided their nests for eggs. I grew clever at hunting. I even made snares out of vines and goat hair, and caught rabbits. I sharpened a long three-pronged stick, and sometimes I could prong fish when they came into the shallows. There were crabs and mussels and periwinkles in the seaweed at low tide, and cockles to dig. After I found a piece of flint on the beach, I could even make fire and cook my food. I knew how to make fire with flint and steel—I had my flint and I had my knife.

At first it was hard, but as summer went on it got better and better. I learned more and more how to take care of myself. I was free for the first time in my life, and I was happy. If I went hungry some days, it mattered little to me. I even found a cave that I could shelter in when it rained. It was large and roomy once you were inside. I made a bed there of dried bracken, and I shared it with the goat. I shared everything with the goat, everything that I could. He would follow me around, and sometimes I would ride on his back. I waded in the water so much that I learned to swim. I could do whatever I wanted, be lazy and lie in the sun for long days. It was lovely, just lying on my back on the warm rocks with the sun on my face shining in colors through my eyelids. Everything peaceful. Just the soft lap-lapping of the water on the shore, and the gulls crying high overhead. No one there to yell at me or beat me for not working. It was almost like heaven.

There were times when fishing boats passed the island, but then I would hide. At first I was fearful that they were looking for me. Perhaps they were, but the few times that men tried to land on our beach, the goat met them and threatened them, charging at them with his horns, driving them back to their boats. I was proud of him, but worried too that they might do him harm. They seemed afraid of him, though, and the ones he drove off never came back.

It was as if the summer would last forever. But when the cold nights set in and the white frost coated all the twigs and leaves in the morning, suddenly I realized that winter was coming. When I thought about what that meant, I was scared, really scared. I swore I would never go back to Bab Magga; I'd rather have frozen to death. I decided that somehow I would have to survive the winter by myself on the island.

I became frantic trying to find food to store. I was in a frenzy, like a squirrel, running around gathering nuts and apples. I dried mushrooms by laying them on the hot rocks in the sun. I tried to dry grapes, but most of them spoiled and the hornets went mad over them. I gathered the bright red rowan berries, though they were bitter as gall; I knew birds ate them in the winter. I cut hay for the goat and gathered wood. I had no ax, only my knife, but I dragged fallen branches near to my cave and made bundles of twigs and piled them up. I couldn't rest. I felt so desperate that I went sort of crazy with fear of the winter.

Maybe I had been a bit daft off and on all along, being all alone there on the island with only the goat. There were times that summer when I know I wasn't in my right mind. Things happened—uncanny things that I knew couldn't be real—like dreams, but not dreams. I knew they did not have anything to do with Bab Magga's magic, because they weren't horrible or cruel, just very strange and sometimes beautiful and sometimes fun. The first time was when the swans came.

I was lying at the top of a steep bank by the shore when I first saw the pair of great white birds gliding past. I thought they were geese, but I knew they were no ordinary geese. Their wing feathers fluffed up on their backs, the feathers ruffled like curly white wool, and their necks were long and arching. I know now that they were swans, but then I didn't know what to call them. I thought they must be the King and Queen of the Geese, for they were more beautiful and noble than any geese I had ever seen. As I watched, one of them slid ashore into a patch of tall sea grass and disappeared. The other sailed back and forth, waiting, and I watched idly. It was a long time before the first one came back again. I knew there must be a nest hidden in the reeds. I stood up and climbed down the bank into the grass to look for it. I expected the birds to be afraid and fly off when I appeared, but they showed no fear of me. Instead they attacked me! They came rushing back toward me with a great splashing and flurry of wings and water, hissing ferociously, their wild shrieks booming in my ears. I ran in terror, clambering back up the bank out of their reach. I stood there jumping up and down, shouting and throwing sticks at them, but I could not drive them away.

I came back the next day and lay in wait, watching them, but now I was afraid to approach them. They were fierce birds! The King, as I called him, stood guard, beating his wings as he circled in the water. I wanted those eggs. I could taste them already. I tried to think of some way to drive him off.

It came to me during the night, when I woke up hungry, that I could steal the eggs out from under the Queen bird in the dark while she was sleeping. I knew by then where the nest was, so I got up and I crept down toward it quietly in the black night, wriggling on my belly through the sharp spiky grass, parting the grass cautiously with my hands. I saw the Queen sitting white on her nest. She was half awake and hissed softly at me as I crept nearer, but she did not stir. I studied her white shape in the dark until I felt I knew where her head was. Then, very carefully, I crept up from behind her and gently reached in under the soft warmth of her feathery body. I felt three large eggs there, warm in my hand, and slowly I drew one out. I knew I should leave one, so she would lay more, so two were all I took. I backed away and escaped safely with my treasure. I managed to climb back up the bank without breaking the eggs, but as soon as I felt safe, I sat up and knocked a hole in one of the shells and sucked out the raw egg. It was delicious and warm, and it tasted so good that I thought of eating the other then and there, but I knew it would be better to save one to eat in the morning.

I woke up hungry and thinking of the egg. In the early dawn I sat up and took the pale green egg in my hands, feeling its smooth shape. I almost hated to break it. I carefully chipped a small hole in the end and then slowly sucked it out, savoring each mouthful. It seemed the most lovely food, like a dream of rich living. It was like having a whole bowl of cream. The sun was coming up blinding white above the trees to the east, and I held up the empty egg between my hands and looked into it. All I expected to see was the sunlight glowing through the empty eggshell.

What I saw was so unexpected that I gasped out loud. At first the egg seemed filled with flowers, tiny bright-colored flowers, and then the flowers drew apart and I saw a garden with a fountain and people—a lady and a little lad sitting on

101

the grass. The little lad held a greenish egg in his hands, like the egg I was holding. The lady reached out and took it and held it to her eye. For a second I saw her face so near that I jumped. I dropped my egg, and it fell to the ground, shattering into bits. Frantically I scrabbled at the pieces, searching for some last glimpse of the magic garden. The lady's face had been so lovely, her hair, her eyes so dark and compelling as they gazed into mine, that I wept at losing that vision. I wept with frustration as I kicked at the small pile of broken shells, grinding them into the hard ground with my heel.

Egg Magic I

EELIE

"What a big egg, Eelie! Where did you find it?" Nana asked me.

"It was here in a nest," I said evasively. I had wanted to see Owen, and the egg was an easy way to do it. I knew he was growing faster than I was, because Raekkin had told me that time went twice as fast in Midgard, where Owen was. I was four and a half, so Owen would be nine years old. But I was surprised at how tall he looked and how thin and wiry and active. It made me think about being active. Maybe . . . maybe it would be fun to run about and climb as he did. There was a wildness about him. He looked uncared for, his hair all wild and shaggy, and his clothes all in rags. I wanted to talk to him, to find out more about him. But Nana came along just then and saw me with the egg.

I thought I would let her see Owen. Even if he was thin

and raggedy, he was a big boy, and it should make her happy to see him. So I gave her the egg and said, "Look inside, Nana. Look what's inside the egg!"

She smiled, as if she would humor me, and took the egg, but she held it doubtfully.

"Go on, Nana!" I urged. "It's special for you."

"I had an Easter egg once," she said in a soft faraway voice. "It was when I was a little girl. I remember, it was like Fairyland inside that egg. Flowers and rabbits and chicks, and so pretty. . . ." Her voice faltered. "How silly!" she said briskly. "Of course this isn't an Easter egg!" And she put the egg up to her eye. "Oh!" she exclaimed. "Oh!" and then almost instantly the egg shattered.

I was angry with Owen, and I wished I could tell him so right to his face. He had broken the egg and broken the spell at the same time.

Nana held the broken bits of egg in her hand, looking very bewildered. "I saw the strangest little boy. Was that one of your tricks, Eelie? Please tell me. I won't be cross, I promise. What was in that egg?"

"That was Owen," I said. "But he's stupid. He broke the egg."

"Owen? Owen in the egg? I *felt* it was Owen, but . . ." She hesitated, and a terrible dark fear seemed to come over her. "Eelie, please tell me. What does it mean? Is Owen dead?"

"Oh, Nana!" I said crossly. She just didn't understand anything. "Oh, Nana, don't be so stupid. How can Owen be dead? He was there, just as you saw him."

"But he couldn't be my Owen. He was so much older. My Owen would still be little, like you are."

"Well, he *is* older! He's twice as old as I am, and he always will be. But even if he's bigger, he isn't as clever as

I am, for it's his fault that the egg broke."

"How can Owen be that much older than you?" Nana exclaimed. "You were born one day before he was!"

It wasn't at all easy, but I *tried* to explain to Nana about the endless worlds all intertwining and all with different time relationships. "You can step into a world and find that a thousand years have passed, or maybe it will be a thousand years ago," I told Nana. "Midgard is the world closest to us. It *almost* overlaps with Erland in space, but time still goes faster in Midgard, *twice as fast.* That's why Owen is older."

But Nana was so disturbed over seeing Owen that she wouldn't even try to understand. In the end I got tired of it. It hadn't turned out at all the way I'd planned, so I gave up and wouldn't say anything more.

It was on a moonlight night while Nana was fast asleep in her bed that I made another egg and talked to Owen. I awoke with bright white patches of light glowing in the dark on floor and furnishings; not plain patches, more like curling feathers of light, more like the patterns on the gowns of the ladies of the court. The light drifted and curled across my bed. The bedspread glowed with a velvety softness, very dark with bright spots of light where there were light spots in the daytime, but the moonspots arranged themselves in circles and formed a different design, different from the old pattern that I knew was there. The light was so bright that I could not sleep. I began to trace the designs on my bedspread with my fingers and play with the light and rearrange it. It was so rich and beautiful that I played with it a long time.

Then I got bored and began gathering the moonlight in my hands, bringing it together and shaping it until it all stayed together in a big, smooth, glowing egg. The egg shone translucent green in my hands in the dark.

I saw the green form into leaf patterns inside the egg, darkening until the leaves were black against a blue-green evening sky. Owen's head appeared over the edge of a bank, his hair all black and tangled standing up every which way, silhouetted against the luminous green. Then he slid down the bank into the darkness. I waited until he had stolen another egg from his swan's nest, and then, when he looked inside, he saw me holding my egg in the dark room.

I put my egg up to my eye, and we were looking at each other. "Come here, Owen, and talk to me!" I said, and though he was scared, he was curious too, and he came. He sat on the bed, and we looked at each other.

Egg Magic II

OWEN

"Come here, Owen, and talk to me!" That's what he said. Just like that, as if it were an order.

It was the second time that I'd had the egg dream. But it was not rightly a dream, because I knew I was awake, and it was not real, because real things don't happen that way. It was some sort of magic, and, as before, it all began with a swan's egg.

I'd been stealing eggs from the nest all along. After I'd sucked them out, I would hold the empty shell up to the sun, hoping to see that strange flower garden again. But the eggshells had all been empty until this night. It was just after sunset, in the green gloaming, that I stole this egg. The full moon was up by the time I had emptied it. I was sitting on the edge of the bank, swinging my legs and looking out to sea. The moon path was wide, a great flashing and splashing of light on the dark waves. The moon was so full and round and bright that I tried holding the eggshell up to its light. This time I saw pictures again! It was like peeping through a small hole into a dark room. A small lad, the same one I had seen before, sat there in a bed holding a green glowing light in his hands. It was an egg! I held my breath. I was very careful not to drop my egg this time. The room I was looking into was all dark except for that green glow. Where was the beautiful lady? I wanted to see her again.

As I watched, the little boy raised the egg to his eye, and then we were looking right at each other, so close that it was hard to keep from jumping back. That was when I heard him say, "Come here, Owen, and talk to me!"

How could I go there? I wanted to. I wanted to see the dark-haired lady again, but knowing it was just a dream or an illusion filled me with misgiving. Before I could decide what to do, all in a breath it was as if I had stepped right into the egg. I was inside an empty pale-green oval room with a curved ceiling overhead—and then the walls dissolved, and before I could get my breath back, I was standing beside the bed where the little boy sat.

"Sit here on my bed, Owen," he ordered. And I did. We looked at each other in the green glow of the egg that he held. He was just a skinny little tyke with eyes that were all pupils in the green light, but his manner was so high and mighty that I wondered at it. He gazed at me intently, studying me, but at least he didn't screw up his nose at me with loathing the way others had.

"Who are you?" I asked. "How'd you know my name?"

"I'm Eelie," he said. "I'm Prince Elver of Erland. Your mother is my nurse. I call her Nana. She still remembers you, Owen, but she thinks you're still a baby!"

"You don't look like a prince," I said. "Where is this place?"

We were in a great lofty stone room, all gloom and darkness except for the moonlight that came glinting in through the windows. "Where are we? Where is my mother? This is just a dream, isn't it? None of this is real, is it?"

"You want to know everything at once!" the little boy said scornfully. He had a funny way of talking, half babyish, half grown-up. "This is Castle Ellorgore. This is Erland. Nana is sleeping in the big bed, but we mustn't wake her. It would scare her to see you, and I'd have to send you back. I want to talk to you and find out about you, so I can tell her about you. You're a prince, too, you know. And Nana is Princess Nora."

"My mother's name was Nora," I said. "How'd you know that? You don't think I'll believe all that talk about princes and princesses, do you? You talk as if you thought I was just a gowk. You're too little to be a prince. You're too little to be ordering people about."

He got sulky. "There's no use explaining things to you. You're stupid!" he said.

"Why should I listen to you?" I said. "You're not even real. You're just a fool dream." And for some reason that made him laugh.

Then he became serious again. "If you don't want to listen to me," he said soberly, "I will listen to you instead. If you tell me all about yourself, I'll not ask questions—or very few questions."

So I told him all about Bab Magga and my father and the goat and the island. It was strange to be talking so much, and all about myself. I had never had anyone to talk to before. I found I was telling him things I had thought I would never tell anyone, all about Bab Magga and the terror I had felt all my life. Even just talking about her made me begin to tremble. I told him about the nightmares I had—the one nightmare that brought the cold dread upon me—where she was coming after me. I would be riding the brown goat. We would be leaping over the crags of a great steep-sided mountain, and she screaming after us on a hairy black goat as big as a cart horse.

He was interested in the dream, but he wanted to hear even more about climbing trees and swimming and hunting. "Those things sound as if they would be fun, but . . ." A strange, unhappy look came into his eyes.

"But what?" I asked.

"I can't do those things," he said. "I can't walk. I can't even stand up by myself."

"Why not?" I asked.

He sort of glared at me, and ignored my question. "Tell me more about Bab Magga and the goat," he said. "Don't you know that the goat is your father?"

"No, he is not!" I stated, feeling angry with him. Was he on Bab Magga's side, too? "Bab Magga tried to make me believe that. But I don't believe it. She's a witch, the worst kind of witch, but she doesn't know how to turn people into animals. She tried to turn me into a toad once, but it didn't work. I stopped believing about the goat after that. I know my father is alive somewhere, and someday he'll find me again. I'll never go back to Bab Magga. I hate her!"

"I know you hate her. I can feel your hate," he said softly, and his eyes were large in the dim room. "Hate is dark purple and red and ugly. It's an ugly feeling. But I understand your hate, because I hate my father the Erl King. It's hard *not* to hate someone who has more Power than you. Unless they love you. Nana loves me, and I don't mind her having Power over me. She would never misuse her Power. But my father turned his Power against me when I was only three years old. That was a terrible thing to do. It was evil!"

When he talked about Nana loving him, I realized that he meant my mother. "Where is my mother?" I asked him. "I want to see her."

He told me to cross the room and pull back the curtain of the big bed. I was fearful but full of curiosity. I wanted to see her, even if it was only a dream. She lay there deep asleep, her dark eyes closed and her dark hair, a black swirling, spread around her on the white sheets. I could believe then that she was a princess, she was so beautiful. I gazed at her calmly. I felt as if my heart were frozen cold and hard as winter ground, and then the tears started, like the first thawing of spring, trickling down. I shivered as I stood there looking at her, filled with longing, knowing this was something I wanted and could never have.

"The moonlight is fading." The small boy's voice broke in on me. "It's turning soft. You'll have to go now, Owen. My egg is getting weak. It's only a moon egg."

I watched my mother fading away as the light grew fainter and mistier. Then everything vanished and I was sitting on the shore of my island staring at the glittery moon path leading out across the black North Sea. I rubbed my eyes with the back of my hand. They stung with salt tears.

Fifth Birthday

EELIE

On my fifth birthday Nana carried me up to see my mother, the Erl Queen. We ate cake and candied fruit, and my mother gave me a new suit of clothes for winter. It was October and already growing cold. There was a fur-lined jacket of dark red wool with bands of gold embroidery that my mother had worked with her own hands. The hat that went with it had a peacock feather on it and a thick fur band around it.

My mother smiled at me and said, "Happy birthday, Prince Elver, my little blue-eyed son." Then she sighed. "This may be the last birthday I will celebrate with you."

Her sigh was like silver frost in the room. I wished that she had not sounded so sad, but I only said, "I like the clothes. Thank you, Mama." I was very much in awe of her because she was so pale and beautiful and mysterious, but I knew I was supposed to call her "Mama," so I did. There had been a remoteness about my mother lately, a withdrawing as if behind a veil of transparent ice. The warmth of her love could no longer shine through. I knew Nana had always felt this cold. Now I felt it, too.

The King also sent a gift. It was a great scroll of parchment that Raekkin read to me, all about fiefdoms and domains. It was very boring to have to listen to all that, and I thought it a pretty poor sort of present.

My mother didn't eat any of the cake, and she let us take what was left back to the nursery. Raekkin came, and he brought his friend Grypyr, the Keeper of the King's Stables. Grypyr was very tall and strong, with blazing flame-blue eyes. His long hair was tawny gold and his beard red, like sun and fire together. I was impressed wih Grypyr. Menia brought us a pot of hot spiced glug and everyone got merry. We all ate more of the cake; even the jackdaw had some.

"Jack-a-dandy!" he cried, begging for crumbs. "Jack-a-dandy likes plum cake and sugar candy!"

It was such a big cake there was still almost a third of it left after everyone had eaten all they wanted. Nana said I would be sick if I ate any more, so she put it in the moon cupboard that hung high on the wall. She said it was to keep it safe from Jack, but I knew it was really so I couldn't get at it.

Nana gave me a pair of blue stockings and mittens that she had knitted, and Raekkin and Grypyr brought me gifts, too. Grypyr was very mysterious about his gift. He held out his empty hands to me and said, "This is a Spirit Slayer, Prince Elver. It is an invisible sword."

"What does it look like?" I asked. "What is it for?"

"It looks like flame," Grypyr said. "It will protect you from evil spirits. If they should ever attack you, you can hold them off with this weapon, for if it touches them, they will dissolve into mist."

"May I hold it?" I asked. "Or is it just make-believe?"

"You know better than that," Grypyr said reproachfully. "Would I give you a make-believe sword? No, it is real, as real as flame, but like flame it will remain invisible until you call it into being. When you need it, it will be there if you say its name. The name is Vegandi. Don't forget!"

I thanked Grypyr for his gift, but still it wasn't much fun to have a sword that I couldn't see, and I didn't have any evil spirits to try it out on.

I liked Raekkin's gift best of all. He gave me a magic bowl. I knew it was magic because it had birds and fishes and rabbits painted on it in pretty colors, and when I looked in it, I could see the birds flying and the fishes swimming and the rabbits running.

Raekkin said, "This is the Bowl of the Peaceful Earth. The runes written around the rim spell out the charm song of this bowl. All you have to do is turn the bowl and say the words and ask for whatever you need. But do not waste the magic. You must use it wisely. Someday, when you are hungry and cold, this bowl will save your life."

I knew it was a very special gift, but I just liked looking at it. I wasn't in a hurry to use it, because I was afraid that if I asked it for something good to eat, I would end up getting porridge or turnip mash. That would probably be the bowl's idea of what I *needed*. Some magic things were like that. They had minds of their own.

That night I was very tired but too excited to sleep. I lay awake long after the fire had died down and the room began to get cold. Just thinking about the cake in the cupboard made me hungry again. I sat up in bed and studied the cupboard door. Why not try to open it? There was a moon cutout in the cupboard door, and I thought about that moon in a green wood, about the door being an opening in the trees with the moon shining through. I thought about trees and leaves, until the cupboard began to shimmer and turn green and glow. The door was slowly swinging open.

I slid down off the bed and crawled over to the cupboard on my hands and knees. It was hard work even to crawl that far, but I was determined to get that cake. I looked up at the cupboard. It was so high on the wall I could not even *see* the cake—all I could see was the green luminous mist that filled it.

My thoughts reached out for the cake and gently lifted it from the shelf. I held it suspended in the air, feeling the heavy weight of it. But I began thinking about how good it would taste, and that was a mistake. Suddenly it slipped from my mind's grasp.

Smash! It fell to the floor and broke up!

But that didn't matter. I sat there and started eating the broken pieces, one after the other, until I wasn't hungry any more. I thought of Owen and wished he were there to help me eat the cake. It would be his birthday, because Nana had told me he was born the day after I was born. Owen wouldn't have a cake. I thought about Owen and the things he did. I wondered what it was like on his island. Visiting Owen might be more fun than having him visit me.

That was when I decided I'd take the rest of the cake to Owen. I held the cake in my lap—there was still a great big chunk of it left—and I stared at the open cupboard, still shimmering and green inside. I kept staring, and slowly it began to *turn inside out*. It turned to gold and russet mixed with sunlight and shadows, and then autumn leaves were spinning and falling all around me, and I was sitting on the ground in a wild woodland in Midgard.

October Visit

EELIE

It was morning already in Midgard. The yellow leaves fell like a star shower flickering down in the bright morning sunlight. I had never been in a wildwood before. It was very different from the garden at Ellorgore, where all the trees were pruned into neat shapes. I had never seen so many trees so close together and so tangled up, their trunks twisting and running upward, disappearing into gold and russet leaves all thick overhead. A starling's notes rang out sweet and clear nearby, and I heard the shrill chattering cry of some small animal. All I had on was my nightshirt, but the air was so warm that wisps of steam were rising from the tree trunks wherever the sun's rays fell.

But where was Owen? I looked around. All I could see was trees. His island was bigger than I had thought.

Then I heard the chattering, scolding cry louder and closer.

A small furry animal was sitting in a tree flicking his bushy tail up and down in short jerks. His whole body quivered as he shrieked at me. I stood up to see him better, and he turned and scurried away right up the tree trunk, and then leaped through the air, landing with a crackling rustle of leaves on another branch, and disappeared.

"Ratatosk?" I called. "Is that you, Ratatosk?"

"Is *who* Rat-a-tat-too?" a voice asked.

It was Owen. He stood there holding a wicker basket and looking like a wild thing, as if he would turn and run if I made the least move. But he wasn't really afraid, because he came forward and stopped about ten feet away and stared at me.

"Who are you?" he asked.

"You know who I am," I said. "I'm Prince Elver. You can call me Eelie—your mother calls me Eelie."

"My mother is dead!" Owen stated flatly. "And you're not real, and I thought you said you couldn't stand up."

"I can't—" I started to say, and then I stopped, speechless with shock. *I was standing! I was standing on my own two feet without holding on to anything!* I felt completely confused. I hadn't even noticed it! I had gotten to my feet effortlessly without thinking. I felt dizzy with the wonder of it. Tentatively I took a step forward, and joy flooded through me. I didn't fall down! I could walk, and it was so easy that I could hardly believe it.

"Look!" I cried to Owen. "Look, I can walk!"

"Ay," he said. "You said you couldn't."

I took a few more steps. My legs were still weak and wobbly, and now that I was aware of what I was doing, it was difficult to balance on them. I swayed as if a wind were blowing me about. But by the time I reached the spot where Owen stood, my legs were straight and strong. I collapsed on the ground and burst out laughing. It was such a marvelous feeling!

"I never could walk before," I said. "Is it magic? Did you do it, Owen?"

"Nay," he said, "I've no magic! It's because you're dreaming. You can do all manner of unlikely things in dreams."

"I'm not dreaming!" I said indignantly.

"How do *you* know?" he asked. "When I was in the castle, I was dreaming. Now you're here, and maybe it's *you* doing the dreaming."

I was impressed in spite of myself, because it was very near to the way Raekkin explained things. I was not in Erland; I was in a different world with different rules. In this world I could walk! I wondered, Would I be able to climb trees too?

"Who were you talking to just now?" Owen asked.

"I was talking to that little animal that ran up the tree. I thought it might be Ratatosk, the squirrel, the messenger. He brings messages from the eagle at the top of Yggdrasill to the dragon at the bottom."

"Ay, it was a squirrel right enough," Owen said. "This is as daft as before. Eagles and dragons! But you're not from Bab Magga, I know that."

"No, I'm not from Bab Magga. I don't even know her, and I don't want to. Not after what you told me about her. Look," I said, holding out the cake. "I brought you some birthday cake. Happy birthday! It's your birthday today. Nana says you were born the day after I was. Here, take it. It's good cake!" And I held out the big piece of cake to him.

Owen put down his basket and took the cake. He took a bite out of it and slowly chewed and swallowed it. "It's really cake!" he said in a wondering voice. "Real cake! And it's good. I never had a whole piece of cake before, just crumbs. Bab Magga used to make cakes when my father was there, but she never let me have any. She said it wasn't good for little boys."

"That's what Nana said, too," I told Owen. "She said I shouldn't eat too much cake or I'd get sick. But I ate lots of it, and I'm not sick at all."

"Here," Owen said. "You can have some."

"No, go ahead and eat it all," I said. "I wanted to bring you the cake, but I really wanted to come see you. Will you show me how to climb trees?"

"I'm gathering walnuts," Owen said. "There's lots of nuts on the ground, but there's lots more in the trees. If I climb the trees, I can shake down more. You could help me pick up nuts."

"I don't know," I said. "I think maybe I would rather climb the tree. Is it hard to do?"

"You're too little," Owen said. "You're just a sprat. But you can help. I've got a cave where I'm storing food for the winter, nuts and apples mostly. Winter is coming on fast, and I have to store enough food so I can live until spring. I've a dread of the winter. I have to gather wood, too, and cut hay for the goat, but it's slow work cutting it, because all I have is a knife. I wish I had sickle and ax and all, but I don't. There's so much to do I can't stop here talking. If you want to help, come along."

"I want to climb trees," I said.

"All right," Owen said reluctantly. "You brought me the cake. I suppose I can show you how to climb a tree."

He led me to a big walnut tree and helped me get started by giving me a boost onto the first limb. He climbed the tree with me, showing me where to put my feet and where to hold on. He pointed out the rotten limbs that weren't safe. I had to *concentrate* hard to keep my legs and arms strong enough to keep on going up. The yellow leaves were beautiful, like a gold ceiling overhead, and as we climbed, it was like going up and up through room after golden room.

I climbed up almost to the top, and then we had to climb down. That was the hardest part. When I looked down, the ground seemed very far away; it was like being up in one of the castle towers.

When we were finally back on the ground, I was glad to sit down. I was really tired. I sat there and watched Owen climb up again all by himself and shake down nuts. It was hard to believe I had really been way up there!

Owen filled his basket with nuts and carried it back to his cave. It was hidden in a rocky hill, and the big brown goat was watching from the cliffside above as we went in through a narrow cleft in the rock, all jumbled and craggy. When we were inside, it was like a big, rough stone room. The floor was crooked, but it was a big enough place, with a low ceiling. There were nuts in one corner and apples in another, and a quantity of wood piled up inside and more wood outside. The wood outside was piled all around a stack of hay.

"That's so the goat can't eat it before winter," Owen said.

"He's not a goat," I told him.

"You keep telling me he's not a goat," Owen said. "But he acts like one. If he's my father, you'd think he'd know the hay was for winter. It's hard to keep him from eating things. I have to keep him out of the cave now. He even eats the baskets. I need a lot more baskets to store things in, but I'll make them later. I haven't got time now. Bab Magga taught me to make baskets. She always said I was a poor hand at it, but at least I know the way of it."

I thought Owen was hard to believe, all the things he did for himself! I knew he was twice as old as I was, from what Raekkin had told me of time going twice as fast in Midgard.

I was five, so Owen must be just ten years old. I wondered if I would be able to take care of myself the way he did when I was ten. I knew a lot, but I had never *done* things. When he went back for more nuts, I was so tired I could hardly drag myself after him. The dry leaves were scrunching and scuffling and rustling about my feet. It was hard to *concentrate* enough to keep up with Owen.

"Gee wug, slowpoke!" he called, going off down the path into the gold and red leafy woods.

I tried to keep up, but he got farther and farther ahead of me. Finally I sat down, just to rest a little. I was sitting there, completely exhausted and beginning to wish I were back home in Ellorgore, when I began to hear voices, soft deep voices, not real voices, strange secret voices.

"*Do you come in peace, Prince of Erland?*" the voices asked.

Somehow I knew they were tree voices. I looked up at the red leaves and red berries of the trees I was sitting under. They weren't leaves and berries—they were really tongues of flame and bright coals burning in the sunlight. It was magic fire, but no magic I had ever met before. It was beautiful, truly lovely. Like all magic, it held deadly danger, but I was too tired to understand or fear it.

"Of course I come in peace," I said fretfully. "But I want to go home now."

"*Come and go in peace, Prince of Erland,*" the trees sighed. "*We are the rowans. We are the Keepers of Peace. Go now in peace. Go softly, go quietly, go safely. . . .*"

It was like the rune song of sleep. The voices swelled and faded, and though I tried to keep listening, somehow I lost them. I must have let go and fallen sound asleep. . . .

. . . I awoke in agony. Nana was shaking me. It was gentle shaking, but it hurt so all through me that I cried aloud.

"Wake up, Eelie!" I heard Nana say. "You're having a bad dream."

"No, I'm not!" I sobbed. "It hurts, everything hurts!"

"Where does it hurt?" Nana asked anxiously.

"It hurts all over," I wailed. "It hurts all over!"

She started to pick me up, but terrible pains shot through my arms and legs, and I screamed. I couldn't stop screaming.

"Menia!" Nana cried. "Menia, come here!"

"Look, ma'am," I heard Menia's slow voice. "Look at the moon cupboard. It's blown open, and there's a mess of cake all over the floor."

"That Jack!" Nana cried. "Oh, it doesn't matter. Run and fetch Raekkin. Hurry, Menia, go get Raekkin. Tell him Prince Elver is sick!"

She tried to comfort me, but I just wept. I heard her ask me, "Eelie, love, did you eat *all* that cake?"

"No," I sobbed. "Just most of it."

"Oh, Eelie, dear one, don't cry," Nana said. "Raekkin will make you well."

But I couldn't help crying, it hurt so much. When Raekkin came, he felt me all over, and I screamed when he moved my arms and legs.

"I'll never eat any more cake," I wailed.

"It's not the cake," Raekkin said. He was speaking more to Nana than to me. "There's no pain in his belly. It's his limbs that are hurting him."

"He ate *all* that cake," Nana said. "It must be the cake."

Raekkin began to rub my legs with something that smelled horrible, but I didn't mind the smell; it was just the pain of the rubbing I minded.

But he kept saying slowly and soothingly, "Now just relax, just relax. I'll take away the pain." And he did. The pain seemed to flow right out from under his hands, and then it was gone. I stopped crying then, but I was so worn out that I fell asleep and slept all day.

I was sick in bed a long time. It took a week before the pain and stiffness finally went away. Raekkin never asked me what I had done, but I told him one day when we were alone. I told him about visiting Owen and climbing the tree.

"You did too much at once," he said. "Walking and climbing are excellent exercise, but you've put it off too long. Now your limbs are too weak to obey your will. You must start a little at a time. Start walking around the room just a few steps, and each day do a little more. That is how you will build up your strength. It must be done gradually, not all at once. Then your body will do whatever you order it to do. But you need a strong body to match a strong will."

"I'll never walk or climb again," I said fiercely.

But although I meant it at the time, I just couldn't keep from thinking about Owen and his island. So when I finally felt well again, I started trying to walk as Raekkin had advised me, a little bit more each day. I really tried, but no matter how hard I concentrated, it just didn't work. I would get to my feet and stand up holding on to something, but as soon as I let go, my legs would go all weak and just collapse under me. I would get angry and tearful, and it didn't help when Nana would say, "You could do it, Eelie, if only you were more *determined.*"

Raekkin taught me exercises to strengthen my limbs. I learned to do somersaults and even to stand on my head. I liked looking at the world upside down. It was almost like the beginning of *turning things inside out.* I still could not stand or walk alone, but the exercises did help; I gradually grew strong enough so I could get about a bit if I held on to someone's arm, and with that I had to be satisfied.

"Why can't I walk?" I asked Raekkin. "I *want* to walk.

Will I ever be able to walk here in Erland? I walked in Midgard. Is Midgard just a dreamworld?"

"It is real," Raekkin told me. "All worlds are real. But in this world something prevents you from walking. Your legs are sound; you will walk eventually."

"But I want to walk *now!*" I cried.

"You have the will. Now you must find the way. Something is blocking your path. Only you yourself can open the way. The answer is somewhere within you. I cannot discover it for you."

But when I looked within me I saw neither way nor door, only blackness. I think that even then I knew what the barrier was, but my eyes would not see and my feet would not walk the path to that dark door.

Wheeltide

EELIE

When December came and the garden was all covered with snow, Nana bundled me up in furs and carried me outside. There she would push me about in a little sled shaped like a boat. That year I was five years old, I was suddenly more aware of everything. It was beautiful when the snow fell tumbling down, swirling like a thick white shower of blossoms covering the garden. All the towers and battlements of the castle looked like my birthday cake covered with white icing. The fountain in the garden did not spray any more, but all the marble frogs and mermaids and sea horses changed their shapes and became ice trolls. The ravens were everywhere, walking up and down the white paths.

It was a sad time, too, for my mother, the Erl Queen, lay dying. She was too sick even to see me any more. In the white garden I felt that the quiet was different from what it had been. It was as if everything held its breath and waited for the end. Nana felt it, too, and seemed to grow more thoughtful. It was as if we both grew older in our minds and put childish chatter aside.

The garden was ice-cold and empty, except for the black ravens who made their dismal croaking noises, and the wind that crawled around, rattling the branches of the bare, lifeless trees. I didn't like the ravens. There were too many of them, more than I had ever seen before, and their croaking was different. If you listened you could hear that they were chanting a song, a black wind song, like the coldest cold you could ever know:

> *Hugin and Munin call us and we come*
> *From the far worlds of space.*
> *We come on black wings*
> *Through the cold, endless night between the stars.*
> *Death comes as we come.*
> *Death takes as we take,*
> *Of the flesh and the bone and the eyes.*
> *On the flesh we feed our flesh.*
> *Of the bones we build our worlds.*
> *We take the stars from the eyes*
> *To brighten the emptiness*
> *Between the far distant worlds,*
> *As they whirl, as they weave through space.*

I didn't like the ravens' song. But Nana did not seem to hear it. There were a lot of things she just didn't seem to be aware of.

But even though Nana did not understand the words of the ravens, she did seem to feel that the garden was different this winter. "All those ugly black birds," she said. "Let them have the place if they want it!"

She began to take me instead to the inner courtyard where the stables and workshops were. I liked that part of the castle with all the clanging and noise and activity.

There were lots of things to see and learn about. Fires blazed in the forges where blacksmiths hammered at the glowing red iron, the hammers sending up showers of bright sparks with each blow. In the armory the armorers clanged away, too, hammering at the steel armor plate, shaping it into battle gear for the knights to wear. There were other workshops, too: cobblers and leather-workers and harness-makers.

In the stables the great horses stood in long rows in their stalls, munching their hay and oats and stamping their hoofs. Milk cows, too, were stalled in low sheds built against the castle wall. Nana loved the sweet smell of the cows, for it reminded her, she said, of her own cow barn back in her faraway home.

Nana carried me about and showed me all that was going on. I loved the great tall horses. I would hold on to their manes and beg to be lifted up on their backs, and often Grypyr, the Keeper of the King's Stables, would take me up in the saddle before him and ride me about the courtyard, the horse's nostrils puffing steam into the cold air and the great iron-shod hoofs clanging and striking sparks from the cobblestones.

I liked Grypyr, but not only because he was Raekkin's friend and had given me Vegandi, the Spirit Slayer. He was both strong and wise. He knew all about horses and would answer all the questions I asked. He told me about the great white horse Ornhest that was the King's own horse, the swiftest horse in the whole stable and also a Water Strider. He was a Sky Horse, too, and the one that the King always rode on the Wild Hunt. I listened to stories of the Wild Hunt that Grypyr told me as he rode me around the courtyard. The Wild

127

Hunt was magic, and its secrets were not for Nana's ears or just anybody's ears—as Ornhest was not for just anybody to ride, only the Erl King.

Grypyr knew all about weapons and armor. He explained about the different kinds of weapons the armorers were making. There were bills, oxtongues, poleaxes, and glaves. All of them different, and those were just the pole arms. There were all kinds of swords and battle-axes too, each with a different name and different use, and there were maces and morning stars. Grypyr told me about the old kings and heroes. He didn't think I was a baby, as Nana did, and he didn't talk as if everything were a lesson, like Raekkin.

A lot of things that Grypyr told me were very mystifying. Once he said, "In a future time, when I am old and white-bearded, I will live in a house built high on a mountain crag. Eagles will fly in and out of my rooms, and you will be one of those eagles."

It made me think of flying like an eagle high up in the mountains, and I liked the thought.

I told Raekkin I liked Grypyr's stories. "Why don't you tell me about battles and heroes?" I asked.

"Grypyr has his knowledge, and I have mine," Raekkin said. "I am a man of peace. If you want to learn about war, listen to Grypyr."

"Grypyr says the first battle in the world was fought with stones, and the last battle will be fought with Fire of the Gods. Grypyr says he has seen that last battle. How can he see a battle that hasn't happened yet?"

"Grypyr sees the past and he sees the future," Raekkin said. "He has the Gift of Sight. If you don't understand what he says, just listen and remember. Someday you will achieve understanding." He looked at me thoughtfully. "Tomorrow is Wheeltide," he said. "Tonight is the Mother Night, December twenty-first, the longest night in the year. The birth is tomorrow. Grypyr and I intend to ride out tomorrow to see the Wheeltide festival. Would you like to come with us, Prince Elver? You'll have to get up early."

I said, yes, I'd like to go. I knew about Wheeltide, although I had never seen it. A festival sounded like fun, and riding horses was always fun. I was happy at the thought of *doing* something.

We rode out in the cold dawn—right outside the castle. I had looked down from the high battlements often, but this was the first time I'd actually gone outside. Grypyr set me up before him on the great black horse Helfaxi, and Raekkin rode on his black mare, Midnætti. Both horses wore harnesses of red with many brass knobs, and gold tassels dangling. We rode out the South Gate, and we were in the little town of houses with straw roofs, all built on the rocky hillside below the castle wall. All the houses were so ramshackle they looked as if they would tumble down into the icy lake if a strong wind blew. The narrow crooked streets of the town were all slushy and crowded with people dressed up in bright-colored clothes, wearing masks and carrying lanterns on poles, and funny things like fishes and bunches of holly and cocks' tail feathers, everybody pushing and jostling one another.

"Why do people live out here and not in the castle?" I asked Grypyr.

"They're fisherfolk. They live here near their boats." He pointed down the hill, and I could see the boats with the fan-shaped nets moored there near the dark docks.

There was one wide street in the middle of the town that ran down to the water, and soon we came to where the street started. We sat on our horses and watched men tying straw onto a great wheel that was lying on the ground. We waited, and I could sense the tension in the air. It seemed to throb and twang. There was a quivering of Power around us, as if the air were alive and vibrating.

When the wheel was all tied up with straw, the men pushed and heaved it up on edge and held it there with long poles while one man set fire to it. The straw started smoking and blazing. I felt the Power glowing deep in the wheel itself. As soon as the whole wheel was on fire, they gave it a great push and sent it rolling over and over straight down the hill. Fire and sparks were streaming from it as it went hurtling downward. The fiery wheel made a great leap as it neared the water and went sailing through the air. It crashed into the lake with a great hissing and a cloud of steam rising.

I watched the steam cloud drifting and shimmering across the lake, and the whole world was hushed, silent and waiting for something. Then Raekkin pointed.

"There it is," he whispered, and his voice held both reverence and darkness. "There it is, the New Born!"

And at that moment the bright disk of the sun rose dazzling white over the dark forest at the lake's edge, and a cry went up from the watchers.

As we rode back through the town, we met a small cavalcade—the Erl King riding on Ornhest accompanied by his gentlemen.

"Ho!" the King shouted as we reined up. "Here's my son, Prince Elver!" His shout was like an ax cleaving the air. "So you've crawled out of your shell for Wheeltide! Well, little *wizzago*, tell me, what did you see?"

I knew he was mocking me, but I tried to answer. I was still spellbound with the wonder of the Wheel—it had been so beautiful, wild and burning. It had been more than beautiful. It had been magical in a way I could not grasp. I still felt the magnificence of it, the dazzling power—spinning, alive, whirling with mystery. I was still overwhelmed, still filled with terror and delight. I drew a deep breath and tried to say it in words. All I could say was, "It was a big wheel on fire—the biggest wheel in the world—and it went splash into the water!"

The King looked at me with an incredulous, glaring look, and then he laughed. I could feel the scorn in his laughter, like thorns drawing blood.

"Is the brat weak-witted as well as weak-spirited?" he asked over my head. "Master Grypyr, Master Raekkin, you've not made much of a work of him, have you? Perhaps you did not have enough to work with. May the gods give me sons yet! I could do with better than this witless bit of spittle!"

I felt myself getting all hot inside and out. But I did not answer. I wanted to show him I was not afraid, but I *was* afraid. I *dared* not answer him. I shrank back tight into my innermost center of being. Someday, I thought, someday I will show you what I am!

The King rode off on his way, laughing with his men, and Grypyr and Raekkin and I turned back toward the castle.

"Prince Elver," Grypyr said. "Didn't you see the Sun Chariot, with the Sky Horses Alsvinn and Arvak pulling it?"

"Don't tell him what he saw or didn't see!" Raekkin shouted at him. "When his eyes are open, he'll see. Now he is as a hooded hawk!"

"*A hawk!*" Grypyr said coolly. "It's plain you're no falconer! You'll be calling a gyrfalcon a kestrel yet!"

"I can tell a hawk from a hernshaw!" Raekkin was still shouting.

"Then learn your eaglets!" Grypyr answered.

I could tell that the two of them did not agree about something, but what it was I did not know. They should have been angry at the Erl King, not at each other. But neither of them said another word on the ride home.

When we got back to the stables, Grypyr told me, "Watch carefully when the horses are unsaddled and unbridled. Someday you will have to do that for yourself."

Raekkin grunted, which meant he was in agreement with Grypyr again. "Which horses are you racing on the Feast of Horses?" Raekkin asked. That showed he wanted to make amends, because he wasn't really interested in horses.

"I've three good colts," Grypyr replied. "But there'll be no racing. There'll be a Departing instead."

Raekkin looked troubled. "That's when it's to be then, is it? I've held it off these five years. But there's no more I can do—not I or any other."

"Ay, I know," Grypyr said, and added, "There's to be a departing in more ways than one."

"How do you mean?" Raekkin asked sharply.

But Grypyr just looked at me and at Raekkin and shook his head, which meant he didn't want me to know.

I rode on Raekkin's shoulders back through the castle corridors. My arms were around his neck, and I leaned my cheek against his shaggy head. It was comforting, like a bear rug.

"I know what Grypyr meant by a Departing," I whispered in his ear. "He shouldn't try to keep secrets from me. It's my mother the Queen, isn't it?"

"He only meant to spare you sorrow," Raekkin said gruffly.

"She's going to die soon, isn't she? I've known it a long time."

"Yes," Raekkin said. "You've heard the ravens. They've been gathering since snowfall. But they are not ravens."

"Even Nana doesn't like them," I said, "though she doesn't hear the words of their song. It's funny that she doesn't understand them. She talked to Munin once. She told me."

"They are not ravens," Raekkin repeated. "They have come for the Departing. It will be five days from now, on the Feast of Horses. That is what Grypyr meant. He can see the future."

"Why does my mother have to die?" It was something that puzzled me. Why should she die if she was a Shape Changer? "Why can't she just change herself into something that will live forever?"

"All living things die," Raekkin told me. "Even the gods must die. There is nothing that lives forever. Though a tree may live for three thousand years, still it must die as surely as a rose that lives only a day. Even if the Queen became such a tree, she would still be stricken, broken and shattered as by lightning, sickened by blight, rotted in her own heartwood. Still she would die. None of us can turn aside death."

"What has blighted my mother? Why has she been sick all these years?"

"Ah, if I knew that, perhaps I might have made her well again. But her sickness has been a mystery to us all, to all the wisest physicians, to all the most powerful sorcerers. None could help her."

"My father the King, he is the Master of Magic. Could he not save her?"

Raekkin shook his head. "He least of all," he said.

That chilled my heart. I could not bring myself to ask Raekkin what he meant. It could only mean that my father would not save my mother, even if he could. She was dying. Was it *because* of him she was dying? The thought terrified me. I felt again the sickness of hatred, a blackness I could not face. Raekkin could not see my face, but I knew he must see the horror that I glimpsed. Yet all he said was, "Queen Elva will not mind dying."

By then we had reached the nursery, and we didn't talk

about death there. But I thought about it. I loved my mother, but not the way I loved Nana. I was sorry for her and had been for a long time. I was glad she would be free. She would cross the golden bridge over the River Gjöll into the Land of the Dead. Maybe there she would find a true king to love her as my father did not.

Winter Visit

EELIE

The excitement of Wheeltide, the meeting with my father, the foreboding of death—all these things made me restless. I was tired of lessons. I was even tired of visiting the courtyard, because I couldn't *do* anything. I could only watch other people doing things. When I saw two stable boys throwing snowballs at each other, I decided it might be fun to visit Owen again. In Midgard I would be able to run and play in the snow like those boys.

I went through the moon cupboard and found that I had come directly to the mouth of Owen's cave. It was lucky that I had, because it was winter in Midgard, too, and everything looked different in the snow. The haystack was all gone and the woodpile, but the brown goat was there under a tree, so I knew it was the right place.

The goat turned his head and looked at me. I would have

liked to talk with him, but I could sense that there were no words in his head, only formless goat thoughts. Still, I felt certain that he was Owen's father.

I had put on my warmest clothes this time, even my fur surcoat over my red jacket. I was glad I had, because it was very cold. A thin trickle of smoke was coming out through the cleft in the rock where the cave was, so I walked up and shouted, "Halloooo, Owen. I'm here. It's me, Eelie!"

Owen stuck his head out. I wasn't sure he was happy to see me. He stared at me, his jaw hanging open. "Gory!" he exclaimed. "You look as fine as fivepence, you do! You look like a real prince this time! Even a feather in your cap!"

"It's a peacock feather," I said.

"A jackdaw in peacock's feathers? I've heard tell of that. Is that what you are?" He grinned.

"No," I said, annoyed. "It's Clootie that's the jackdaw."

His expression changed. The grin vanished and a shadow of terror passed over his face. "Clootie!" he gasped. "That's what Bab Magga called her jackdaw. How'd you know that?"

"I don't know Bab Magga, I keep telling you. But I do know Clootie."

He studied me. "I don't know which of us is dreaming . . . but come inside where it's warm."

It wasn't much warmer inside the cave. There was only a small smoky fire going. The smoke made my eyes water and set me coughing. But the tears didn't matter, because after the brightness of the white snow outside, it seemed pitch-black in there anyhow. Slowly my eyes began to get used to the dark, and now I could see Owen sitting crouched over the small fire. He had on a funny sort of cape all patched together out of small pieces of fur, and straw tied around his feet. He looked pathetic.

"Did you bring anything to eat?" he asked.

"No," I said. "I'm sorry, but I didn't think of it. I just thought I'd come and play in the snow with you." I could see that Owen was thinner than ever, and all the nuts and apples were gone. The cave was very bare. "Don't you have anything left to eat?" I asked. "What became of all the nuts?"

"They're all gone," Owen said. He huddled up close to the fire, shivering and looking miserable. I didn't know what to say. He turned and looked at me defiantly. "It's not so bad. I've got snares set for rabbits. I made my cloak out of rabbit skins. There are still cockles and mussels and periwinkles, but it's cold work gathering them. One day it was so cold that a whole flock of seabirds froze to the ice. I lived high then for a while. The goat is getting thin, but he eats bark and twigs. He'll get by if winter doesn't last too long. It's been an awfully long winter."

In Erland winter was just beginning. But this must be February here in Midgard. Owen *had* had a long, cold winter. I decided I would go back home and bring him something to eat.

"I'll be right back!" I said, and turned and ran out into the snow. I stood looking around at the snowy woods, wondering where the rowan trees were. Everything was all hushed and white. The tree branches drooped down, heavy with snow. The forest floor was all humped and lumpy with strange white snow mounds. Black sticks and branches poked up out of shapeless hillocks. The goat came toward me, going, "Baa-aaa-aaaaaaa." I ignored him.

I had expected the rowan trees to help me, but I couldn't even tell which ones they were. The leafless snow-laden trees all looked the same. I felt a momentary panic.

"I'm stupid!" I said aloud. "I should never have come here. What if I get stuck here and can't get back to Erland?"

I couldn't think what else to do, so I just marched off straight ahead into the white woods. It was so lovely walking through the snow that I lost my feeling of concern. I was elated at my freedom of movement. It was new-fallen snow, light as feathers. Every now and then a mass of it would fall from the trees, and fine icy powder would fill the air. I walked on, following a thin wavering trail. Then the trail ended at a sort of clearing. I could see where Owen had been digging out fallen branches.

I was studying this when suddenly something hit me from behind, a great blow that sent me tumbling facedown in the snow! The breath was knocked out of me. I could only lie there gasping. I felt a sense of shock as someone started jabbing at me with sharp sticks. I raised my head, and there was the goat butting at me with his horns. It hurt, and I shouted at him, "Go away, Eben!"

He stepped backward and shook his horned head at me. I felt his mind filling with red rage. I felt the words inside his head flowing together like molten metal. He flung them at me, spattering and searing hot. "You're one of them! One of the evil ones of Erland! Get off this island, devil, or I'll kill you!"

I was so indignant at him for knocking me down that I couldn't believe I was in danger. The goat took several steps backward and lowered his head to charge. Then I knew he was deadly serious.

"You let me alone, Eben!" I cried desperately, struggling to sit up. "Can't you see I'm trying to help Owen?"

He hesitated, his strange goat eyes staring at me.

"I am not evil!" I said loudly. I put all the Power I could into my words. My words burned like fire in the cold air. *"I am The Helper!"*

For an instant he understood, and I felt the joy flare up inside him. Then he shivered all over. His mind quivered like a candle flame in the wind, and his eyes seemed to go all cloudy. Then there were only goat thoughts there as before.

I was shaken, even surprised, but I was sorry too—sorry I'd had to use the Power, because it had forced his mind to retreat into its goatness. He had been brave. He was defending Owen. If he had not been so weakened by cold and hunger, he could have hurt me seriously, perhaps even killed me, when he first tried to.

Maybe I can help him, too, I thought. But there was no way I could help him. Not then. First I had to help *Owen*. I had to get back to Erland. I knew I wasn't going to get home by wandering around through the snowy woods on this island.

My feeling of panic returned. What if I was trapped here with Owen and Eben? We would all starve to death. Raekkin had warned me that someday I would be hungry and cold and the magic bowl would save my life, but the bowl was back in Erland! . . . *Once I had known real hunger. . . .* When? I reached out and for a brief moment a dark door opened in my mind to reveal a hunger so extreme, so hideous that I slammed the door tight shut and crouched there, in the snow, shuddering, my eyes closed.

I tried to pull myself together. It was necessary to think calmly, but my mind was quivering with terror. *I had to get home!*

"Hugin, help me," I whispered imploringly to the black Raven of Thought.

I felt his soft wing brush my mind. The cool clarity flowed back over me. The answer was etched in the crystal ice-cold beauty of thought. *The way back is through sleep.* It was so simple! When the answer came, it was always beautiful in its simplicity.

The only trouble was that I didn't feel sleepy at all. I remained where I was, my clothes all crusty with snow. I emptied all thoughts of Eben and Owen and everything else out of my mind. I sat there cross-legged in the snow, trying to keep my mind detached. Softly I chanted the rune—the charm song—of sleep:

> Sleep, come to me
> Come as the rain
> Softly
> Come as the snow
> Quietly
> Come as the twilight
> Gently
> Come on the breath of silence
> In the whiteness of nothingness
> Take me to quietness
> To peace.

I got colder and colder sitting there. I never knew when I fell asleep, but I woke up with the smell of burning fir needles and smoke in the air. . . .

. . . There I was, back in my bed in Castle Ellorgore. Menia was putting fir boughs on the coals of the old fire, and sparks were swirling up the chimney. It was morning and the room was cold, the windowpanes all sparkling, thick and furry with frost. I huddled back in my warm featherbed and thought about Owen in his cave.

What should I bring him, I wondered. And it was then that I made the decision to take the magic bowl to Owen. It was just on an impulse, or so it seemed at the time, but I know now that the brief glimpse of my own past hunger through the dark inner door of memory had shaken me, and so had the encounter with Eben.

I knew that Raekkin would understand, but I thought again and again of his words: "Someday when you are hungry and cold, this bowl will save your life." It was a terrifying thought. Was I throwing away my own life in helping Owen?

But in spite of my fears and misgivings I brought the bowl to the cave and taught Owen the secret rune. And Owen actually received all the things he needed so desperately. It was then that I felt the joy of the giving. The feeling was so powerful, so astonishing in its intensity that I knew my name was well-chosen. This was what I was destined to be . . . The Helper of Those in Need.

Though I had called myself Hjälper, I had never helped anyone before in my life. Yet I had not come by my name easily. Raekkin had sustained and guided me on the long search for my *true* name, and even he did not know what it was. Nana was the only one who knew.

The search had been long and arduous. I had journeyed deep into my own inner being, into a weird other world of dreams and nightmares. There I had found not only my *true* name but also the inner Well of Power that I knew I would draw from again and again. I had used that Power to protect myself against Eben. The Power was not to be used lightly. My father had *misused* his Power when he had turned it on me there in the garden, and for that I could not forgive him.

The Bowl of the Peaceful Earth

OWEN

"Hey, Owen!" he shouted. "It's me, Eelie. I'm back!"

He came walking into the cave, holding a big bowl carefully in his hands. I was just building up the fire, and I could see him plainly enough, but he said, "It's too dark in here."

Having the Prince come and go was worse than being alone. I was so near to starving that I knew I would break down and cry if he hadn't brought me something to eat this time. I hated to look at him right then with his fine clothes and his fur-lined jacket.

"We need some light," he said. He stood there, holding the bowl, and began to chant a curious sort of singsong:

> *Birds fly*
> *Fishes swim*
> *Rabbits run*

In the circle of life
Bowl of the Peaceful Earth
Fulfill my needs—
I need light
Give me light!

The bowl began to give forth a soft blue glow. It got brighter and brighter, and while I watched with my mouth hanging open, a great ball of blue fire jumped out and rolled sizzling around the cave, bouncing over the floor and scaring me half witless.

"Damn you!" I yelled. "Get that daft thing out of here!"

He stood there looking as amazed as I was. Then he gave an order in a strange tongue, and the ball stopped spinning around and rose slowly into the air and hung there over our heads, glowing and sizzling still, but at least it was out of our way. It made the cave bright as day.

"That's better," he said, and added apologetically, "It's the first time I ever tried to use this bowl. It's a magic bowl, and magic things are very hard to control."

"I don't need any magic shows," I said bitterly. "I thought you were going to bring me something to eat."

"*You* hold the bowl," he offered, "and say the words. It'll give you anything you *need*. You need food. Go ahead and ask for it."

I wasn't sure I wanted to meddle with his magic. But I was close to starvation, so I took the bowl in my hands and said the words he had said. I didn't remember them right the first time, but he corrected me, and the second time that I tried it the magic worked. The bowl filled up with grain and nuts and fruit, birds flew out of it, and rabbits hopped out and ran around the cave. There were even fishes that spilled out and started flapping about on the floor.

We were both laughing; it was all so daft. But the goat

started pushing up close and reaching out his neck for the food.

"Be careful!" the Prince cried, suddenly sober. "Don't let him break the bowl!"

I emptied the bowl out on the floor and let the goat eat all he wanted, even before I ate anything myself. The bowl filled up again as soon as I emptied it!

"This is beyond all marvelous!" I exclaimed, cramming food into my mouth. "This is the best magic ever."

The Prince looked as happy as I felt. When I'd eased my hunger a bit, I began to consider what else I needed. "Do you think I might ask for a bit of dry firewood?" I suggested. "There's not much left for me to gather."

"If you need wood, just ask for it," the Prince said. "You could ask for a house or even a castle and servants." He was beginning to get excited and carried away, and his eyes were shining. "You could have fine clothes and gold and silver and jewels and all kinds of toys!"

"What would I want with a castle?" I asked. "But clothing and firewood—ay, I could use those."

It was a strange, contrary sort of magic in that bowl. When I asked for firewood, it was as if I saw in a vision a forest of trees that sprang up green all around me, growing higher and higher and then dying, and the dry branches falling on all sides. I sat there mystified, for it did not seem real, and it defied understanding. When the vision faded away, the cave was all cluttered with a jumble of dead wood, twisted branches all piled in a tangle—and real enough to the touch.

We cleared some of it away and tried to pile it up so we would have room. The Prince was panting and sweating. He wasn't used to that sort of work.

"That bowl," he said. "It acts just the way I thought it

would. It has a mind of its own. It keeps overdoing it!"

"You'll not hear me complaining," I said. "Shall I try for the clothing? If I asked for a castle, we'd probably have the roof falling in on us!"

"You do need warm clothes," the Prince said.

So I spoke to the bowl again, and this time four full-grown sheep came bounding out into the cave and ran blatting and blundering among the fallen branches. I couldn't help laughing, and the Prince sat there giggling, too.

"But they're not clothes!" he said when he finally got hold of himself. "Something went wrong that time!"

"There's nothing wrong," I said. "It's often I've wished I had sheep on this island. They're fine, useful animals, and where else would you get cloth but from the wool on a sheep's back? In all truth, I can't say that I ever knitted or wove any cloth or even spun the wool, but I've often watched Bab Magga at it, and I know how it's done. I'll manage to make something of these sheep." I hesitated, not wanting to find fault with the gift. "But there's the matter of feeding them," I said cautiously. "There's little enough for the goat to eat, let alone four sheep."

The Prince smiled happily. "That's no problem," he said. "You'll have lots of food for them. The bowl will provide it. You can keep the bowl, Owen. You need it more than I do. Just don't forget the rune—the magic words—and be careful what you ask for!"

"I'll think a good long while before I ask for anything more. There's little more I could need." And then the truth of it struck me of a sudden. "These marvels won't last. I know that." I felt bitter about it. "It's all a dream, and it's just going to fade away and leave me worse off than before."

But he kept telling me that it was real, that it would last, and I wanted to believe it.

We built up the fire to a fine blaze, and I cleaned and scaled the fish and broiled them over the coals. The Prince was lying there beside the fire, yawning fit to unhinge his jaw and looking sleepy, when all of a sudden he just vanished—like a candle flame blown out in a breeze. One moment he was there and the next he was gone. It scared me thoroughly. I dropped the stick with the fish I was broiling and grabbed the bowl. I didn't want to lose it. But nothing else vanished. The sheep were all there huddled together and blatting, the globe of light was glowing overhead, and the birds were twittering away where they perched among the dead twisted branches. I could even catch a glimpse of the rabbits hiding under the tangle of wood.

I hoped the Prince was all right wherever he had got to. But it did make it all seem even more chancy. I was more than ever in fear that the bowl and all else would vanish any minute. There was one thing I knew I still wanted, but I had not dared ask for it while the Prince was there. I wanted to see my mother.

I sat and thought about it a long time. I held the bowl in my hands and turned it slowly. The pictures on it flowed and changed as I turned it. I hesitated to ask, but the need kept building up in me until I had to act. Once more I recited the charmed words, and then I said, "Bowl, bring my mother to me!"

She came in a vision, not real, but like the trees that had grown and died. I saw her standing on a stone tower, leaning on the wall and gazing out at me. Her dark hair fell straight down on each side of her face, and I could see the tears in her eyes. Then the tower faded, and I saw her in a different place. She was holding the reins of a great white horse, riding slowly up a beach toward me. *It was the beach of this island!* I jumped up, trembling. She was coming.

She was coming home to me! I bolted out of the cave and ran through the snowy woods down to the shore. But when I arrived, panting and breathless, at the edge of the sea, there was no one there.

I sat there on the rocks all day, waiting. It was a warm sunny day, the first warm day in a long time, but I scarcely noticed it then, for my heart was all aquiver and full of hope. As the day wore on and my mother never came, the hope died. I could have cursed the bowl then for bringing me only the illusion of my mother's return.

At last I began to look around me at the melting snow, at the water running over the rocks in rivulets, with the green ferns and moss showing through under the ice. Winter was breaking! There was the sweet smell of wet leaves in the air. It was the beginning of spring in the woods of my island, but it was still deep frozen winter within my heart. Not until the day when I would finally see that horse and rider coming over the horizon, not until my lost mother would actually come riding up the beach toward me, and my father would be there beside me, as we met all three in the circle of each other's arms—only then would my long winter of suffering end.

PART THREE

Departing in More Ways Than One

The Departing

EELIE

"Wake up, Prince Elver!" I dimly heard the words, and then light struck my eyelids as the bedcovers were thrust aside.

"Go away!" I muttered crossly. "Go away. Leave me alone. I'm sleeping!" And I tried to bury my head, but they would not let me sleep. I opened my eyes and came wide-awake in an instant! A tall hooded black figure stood by my bed. More figures, all black with tall pointed hoods, crowded the room, all mixed up with the black shadows cast by torchlight. "Who are you?" I cried, my voice rising in terror.

"Hush, Prince Elver. It's only me. There's nothing to be scared of." It was Menia's voice, and now I could feel that it was her big placid face deep-hidden inside the tall pointed hood of blackness.

"B-b-b-but what is it?" I stammered. "Why are you dressed like that?"

"It's the Departing. We've all to go to the Departing, the Queen's Departing. Come get dressed, do!"

"The Queen!" I was still muddled with sleep. "You mean my mother? You mean she's dying?"

"Oh, no, dear. The Queen's dead. It's the Departing."

"Princess Nora." It was Raekkin's voice now, talking to Nana. He, too, was one of the black hooded figures. "The ceremony is about to begin. As you would call it, a funeral. We call it the Departing. Get dressed now and put on the cloak of darkness. Menia and I will dress the Prince."

I kept rubbing my eyes as they dressed me. I felt very upset. Why did the Departing have to be in the middle of the night? Raekkin lifted me onto his shoulders, but I missed the feel of his hair. The black hood came between us. I didn't like the hiding in darkness.

When we left the room, we found the corridor full of people, a long double line filing past, moving toward the stairs. Each group was led by a linkman carrying a torch. In silence we all climbed the stairs, but not all the way to the top. We came out on the snowy battlements overlooking the lake. It was black and cold and windy up there. Even the wind was black. Raekkin carried me to a place directly over the great gate to the inner harbor. We mounted a high platform, and there stood the Erl King in the windy, snow-spitting dark, dressed all in black, too, with his great gold crown upon his head and his scepter in his hand, as if it were an occasion of state—as of course it was.

Black-robed people—all the inhabitants of the castle—were gathering upon the battlements. The churning lake waters lay below us. Bright moonlight glinted off the dark waves. The tops of the tall towers shone with the white snow that crowned them. The flaring torches cast long shadows in a monstrous moving frieze across the high stone wall behind us. There was a fierceness, a wildness in the night, the north wind blowing the black cloaks and tossing the flames. The wind came whining and moaning, twisting and coiling about the tower corners, sweeping the high battlements and hurling the stinging snow in our faces. I felt half scared, half sorrowful inside, for all about us there was the shrill shrieking of the host of ravens that swirled through the air, and their cries were the death song.

As the people gathered, they, too, burst into keening and wailing and lamentation. I held tighter to Raekkin. I felt all alone and lost in this multitude of mourners, for I alone was unable to weep. I, who had wept for a bumped elbow or a skinned knee, I could not weep for my mother. I could not mourn her going, for I knew it was as Raekkin had said. She went willingly. She set forth on a journey to a new realm. This was her Departing. But though I could not weep, I was shivering, for the cold and the darkness ate at my soul, and the ravens screamed for the feast.

Then suddenly a quiet fell as each black bird lit on one of the stones of the parapet. I was watching as a large raven settled on the merlon directly below me. As it perched there, shuffling its black wings into place, it seemed to swell and grow larger, until it was almost man-size. As it grew, it changed into a grotesque dragonlike creature, half man, half bird, with black silvery scales instead of feathers. I had seen carved demons of stone, but this one was alive! *They are not ravens*, Raekkin had said. I looked about me and saw that on each stone merlon a similar figure crouched. Nana was standing nearby. Why wasn't she afraid? I realized then that she was not even aware that the birds had *turned inside out*.

"I don't like them," I said loudly. "Why did they have to come?"

"Hush, Prince Elver," Nana said. "You mustn't talk."

"Oh, Nana! You don't even see them!" I cried. "Look at them! Can't you see them?"

"Silence! Your mother is dead!" The King's loud, harsh voice struck out at me, ripped through me with claws of darkness. It made me jump! I had forgotten he was so near.

How could I forget his presence? Now my thoughts rushed out like scouts into enemy territory, exploring, probing his feelings. What was it like, his grief? And my scouts came hurrying back like frightened hares plunging safe again into my mind, but bringing with them a terrible intelligence. It was not grief they had found, but a fierce and dreadful joy, a terrible exultation, a fearful glee! My father was rejoicing, rejoicing in this Departing, in my mother's death, in his Queen's death. He was glad!

His great voice rang out again, tolling like a bell through the silence. "Let the Queen depart!"

I was trembling, like the rabbits of my thoughts. I tried to scrunch down tighter, burying myself in the blackness of Raekkin's hood, crawling into a dark safe hiding place. In the silence we all heard the creaking and clanking of heavy chains. Inch by inch the great gate rose. Then a long dark ship glided out through the gate below, slowly out into the lake.

The ship was almost invisible, but we could feel its passing. It moved like a shadow out into the black night, and we would not have seen it at all except that it followed the bright moon path. The black shape of the ship sliced a blackness out of the sparkling light on the waves as it moved smoothly and silently on its journey. Far out into the center of the lake it sailed. No sails or oars were visible, only the empty mast and the tall curved prow with its black dragon's head.

"That boat . . ." Nana breathed. "I remember that boat!"

Then, as we watched, a sudden bright flame licked out along the gunwales, swiftly circling the craft. I trembled. I felt like screaming then! But there was complete silence from the watching crowd. The fire spread, climbing the mast and flaring from the rigging. Then the whole ship burst into flame and roared up bright against the darkness, sending a mass of flame and sparks streaking up high into the black night. The ship burned down to the waterline as we watched. I knew the Queen's body was on board that dark craft. I felt as if the flames ate at me, too, consumed me, charred my bones, reduced me to gray ashes. There was little left of me. I was nothing but a bit of gray dust blowing on the black wind.

Then the King's voice boomed out again. "It is done! Go take your rest, my Queen!" He turned on his heel and marched down the steps and strode off into the night.

No one stayed any longer. The crowd broke up and we all returned to our rooms. Raekkin carried me back and helped put me to bed.

"Now, my Prince," he said, bending over me. "Now you know what a Departing is. A Departing is by fire!"

"Why is it by fire?" I asked. "I didn't like the fire!"

"A Shape Changer's Departing is always by fire—so that the spirit can go free."

"I am glad my mother is free," I said carefully, but somehow I had a rather unhappy feeling about it. My father's gladness, his terrible gladness, made me doubt that I was glad at all.

Nana leaned over and kissed me and tucked me in. I could feel that she was unhappy about it, too, perhaps because she didn't understand about death. I wasn't sure I really understood either. I didn't want Raekkin to go. I wanted him to stay and talk to me.

"I didn't like the fire, but at least the ravens can't eat her," I said. I was near tears.

"They were not ravens," Raekkin said. "They were the Demons of Flight. They have come on the thirty-two winds of the sky, from all the far worlds, to honor our dead Queen."

"Will they depart again?" I asked anxiously. I was not at all happy at the thought of their staying.

"They will depart," Raekkin said, "as they must."

"Is that what Grypyr meant by a *departing in more ways than one?*"

"Go to sleep!" Raekkin said gruffly. I knew then that Raekkin was grieving. He alone was truly grieving, and I loved him for that, almost as much as I loved Nana.

I will ask Grypyr, I thought. But I forgot. Sleep nuzzled me gently and then gulped me down into its warm maw. I forgot all about it. I forgot what I was going to ask Grypyr.

A Proposal

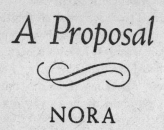

NORA

We lived quietly in the winter stillness of the nursery, and Prince Elver studied with Raekkin. The white snow fell day after day, drifting and piling high, covering the nursery windows, sealing us in. Only the tops of the tall windows were clear enough to let in the dazzling snow light. The wolves howled at night and swept in packs across the frozen drifts on the lake, so that sometimes of a morning we would see their stark gray shadows passing across the walls of our room. There were days when, as we sat around the fire, we would roast on the front and freeze on the back of us, and the fine snow, leaking in the edges of the iron casements, piled up in white drifts across the floor.

Together we pored over the beautiful books, reading the tales of gods and giants and dwarfs. We read of Iduna sleeping under the white wolfskin of winter, in the cold and dark of Niflheim, while the world waited for her to return and bring the flowers and green of spring. So we, too, waited for the end of winter.

It came at last. First the pouring rain and melting slush, then the reviving sun, unfurling buds on every bush and tree, and the small birds singing in the new green of the garden.

One day when I came in from the garden carrying Eelie in my arms, I found a herald waiting for me, and two elegant ladies of the court as well. The herald greeted us formally and proceeded to unroll a scroll of parchment and read forth a proclamation. It began: "Know ye all men by the power herein invested in me, that I, King Elrik of Erland . . ." and it rambled on through wherefores and whereafters and whereases until I was completely confused. I listened politely, but Eelie grew impatient.

"I do not understand any of that," he stated. "And I'm sure Nana doesn't either. Why don't you just tell us what it's supposed to mean!"

The herald looked flustered, but finally after much throat-clearing he said, "It means the King wants to see Princess Nora so that she may listen to a royal proposal. That's what it means!"

The two ladies tittered and told me I should be honored to be summoned to an audience with the King. They proceeded to instruct me that I must dress in my finest clothes. They had brought a small carved box, a present from the King. In it were two great ropes of pearls that they said were for me to bind in my hair.

It was quite unexpected for me to receive so much attention, but Eelie said, "You're a princess, Nana. He should have invited you to the court long ago!"

If Eelie was pleased, then I was. So I dressed, with the help and advice of the two ladies-in-waiting. I put on an embroidered gown that Queen Elva had given me, and they helped me to dress my hair and bind it with the pearls. They then escorted me to the throne room.

I had never even seen the throne room before. It was a grand lofty hall, the ceiling of shimmering gold and the floor of polished stone. The walls all hung with tapestries, and with many banners on poles—yellow and blue and red designs of dragons, boars, and running horses, as well as runes and cabalistic emblems enough to confound the eye. This hall was filled with noblemen and ladies, all in the richest and most colorful garments. The herald marched in front and led me down the center of the hall with the two ladies-in-waiting following. At the far end the Erl King sat on a throne high on a dais. For the first time I felt like a princess. I held my head up and walked with stateliness, and my heart was light.

As we approached, the herald stopped and blew a long blast on his trumpet. Then he announced me: "The Princess Nora of Strathclyde in Midgard."

The King's voice boomed out. "Come along up here, my dear. Don't be shy."

Behind the King's throne hung tapestries of battle scenes. As I approached the throne, I gazed at the intricate violence, at armed men and horses clashing and tangling together, with bits of dismembered limbs and severed heads strewing the ground. The two ladies behind me leaned forward and whispered loudly, "Kneel down! Kneel down!"

So I knelt there at the foot of the throne.

"Get up!" the King ordered. "Come up here and let me see your pretty face!"

The words seemed cheerful banter, but something was not right. There was an ominous quality in his voice, a heaviness not in keeping with his words. I rose and climbed the steps of the dais until I stood directly below him. He leaned over, his broad ugly face peering down at me, his legs wide astraddle with his hands resting heavily on his knees. His power hung over me oppressively. I felt the dead weight of those fierce eyes. They were of a strange golden hue, sunk in the massive head. The coarse gray beard encircled the heavy chin, and his skin was mottled gray and lumpy with warts. I could not bear to look upon his face, so I looked at his hands instead. They, too, were grotesquely knobbed and warted, with rings deeply imbedded in the graying flesh.

"Well, my dear," he said, "no doubt you're wondering why I've called you here." The heaviness of his voice weighed on me like stone. I began to feel that I could scarcely breathe. "I've decided to make you my Queen. Does that please you, eh?"

I raised my eyes to his and saw the baleful glint in them. I could not speak. I knew then that I loathed him. The flesh on me crawled. The soul in me crawled and groveled before him. And for that I hated him, for he made me hate myself.

"I'm offering you marriage!" he roared, enraged by my blank stare. "Well, woman, where's your tongue?"

I found my tongue. "I cannot marry you!" I blurted out.

The baleful glint was no longer a glint. His eyes glowed openly and ferociously.

I took a deep breath and tried to speak more formally. "Indeed, Your Majesty, I thank you for the honor you do me," I said stiffly. "But I cannot accept your offer, for I am already married."

"You are no longer married!" the King stated ominously. "You're a widow! Your husband is dead—or as good as dead!"

My heart had almost stopped at the word "dead," but the last of it took the terror from his words.

"If he's only *as good as dead*, I am not a widow," I said. "And if he *were* dead, I would want proof!"

The Erl King grinned then. His teeth gleamed in his great maw. "I'll tell you what I mean by *as good as dead.* Your husband is no longer a man. He's a goat! You're married to a goat! Does that count as a marriage? Not even in Midgard can a woman claim she is married to an animal!"

I was hot now and flushed with anger. "You're mocking me! My husband is alive, and I'll hold to that until I see proof otherwise!"

His look was pure evil now and dark as a lowering storm. "You want proof, do you? Well, a goat can be killed easier than a man!"

"You may kill all the goats you like," I answered, but I was uneasy at the thought. "It can't be!" I cried out. "It can't be! Perhaps you can change people into animals here in Erland, but not in my world. Things like that don't happen there!"

"They happen with Erlish help," the King said, the ominous darkness deepening in his voice. "Shall I put it to the test? Shall I send to Midgard and have them kill a certain brown goat and bring its head here? What then, my lady? What if that head turns out to be the head of your husband? How will you like that, knowing you ordered his death?"

I was sick with this game. I knew now he was just tormenting me. All I could say was, "I cannot marry you. I am already married."

He glared at me. "You're a stubborn bitch! There's only one proof of wedlock that means anything here in Erland. If your marriage is valid, your gold ring will still be bright. If your marriage is over, your ring will be tarnished as brass."

Instinctively I clasped my hands. "I've lost my ring," I whispered. "My jackdaw stole it."

He leaned back, grinning widely. "Your jackdaw! Your jackdaw stole it! Your jackass, more likely. I can be stubborn too, my lady! I could have had a hundred fairer maids than you, but it's you I've said I'll marry, and it's you I will. I'll give you until tomorrow to find your ring. If you cannot discover it, then we'll announce our betrothal, eh, Princess Nora!"

I knew I could never find my ring, but before I could say more, the King turned and shouted, "Here, Herald! A proclamation! Princess Nora will be my bride, unless by tomorrow she finds the wedding ring that she claims to have lost."

Then abruptly he rose to his feet and bellowed like a bull, "You can go back to your nursery, my lady, until tomorrow!"

I turned, near blinded with the tears of my anger, and started down the long hall. A shocked murmur arose from the crowd of nobles. One of the ladies-in-waiting rushed forward and tried to turn me around. "You must not turn your back on the King!" she whispered fiercely. But I shook her off and walked on down the long hall.

I was trembling so with rage that I felt and saw nothing. I went in a blindness of spirit through those stone corridors, the tears held back only by force of will. By the time I reached the nursery, I was ready to sit down and cry. But I had no chance for that. Almost as soon as I entered the room, Raekkin and Grypyr arrived. They stood there—the heavyset dwarf and the tall horseman—"the long and the short of it" I had often called them to myself. Now I was more than glad to see them, but it was not good news or comfort that they brought.

"We have come to say good-by, Prince Elver," Raekkin said, addressing the small Prince.

Eelie sat up and frowned. "Good-by?" he asked. "Where are you going?"

"King Elrik has ordered us both to leave Ellorgore," Raekkin said. "He has banished us to the Mountains of Hraesvelger."

Eelie looked stunned. "He can't! He can't do that! He can't send you away. Why does he want to do that?"

"I'm afraid he does not like our advice," Raekkin replied. "We advised him, Grypyr and I, not to persist in his plan to marry Princess Nora."

"Marry Nana! He can't do that!" Eelie cried, his voice rising.

"No, Eelie," I said as calmly as I could. "He cannot marry me, for I am married already."

"It is dangerous to thwart a king," Grypyr said. "We will be safe enough in the mountains, but I wish you well, Princess Nora."

"He's a bad man! He's a bad man to want to marry Nana and to send away my best friends! You are my best friends!" Eelie's voice was shaking. "When I am King, I will send for you!" he announced. "And if you need help, I'll come to you!"

"When you are King, we will return gladly," Grypyr said.

"I know that." Eelie was sobbing now. "But I don't want you to go!"

"It is best that we go," Raekkin said. "It would not be safe to stay. Farewell then, for now," and he reached out to lay his hand on Eelie's shoulder.

Eelie scrambled to his feet and threw his arms around Raekkin's neck. Grypyr knelt down, and he too was hugged desperately.

Then the two of them turned and said a brief farewell to me and left.

As soon as the door closed, Eelie burst into tears. "I hate him!" he screamed. "I hate him!"

I did my best to soothe him. We clung together, and indeed I could not tell if he was hugging me for comfort or I him. He was almost in hysterics, weeping and raging in turn. I held him in my arms until at last his grief subsided and his sobs grew further and further apart. By then he was so exhausted that I put him to bed, and although it was still broad day, he fell sound asleep at once.

I knew that to lose both Raekkin and Grypyr was a dreadful blow to him, and it was to me as well. I knew now that they had been better friends than ever I had realized. They had risked the King's fury to try to help me. I no longer felt anger or tears. It was a sickness of fear that I felt. If only I could find the ring! It was the one thing that could save me.

The jackdaw sat perched on the windowsill. He had ignored all the turmoil. Now he spread his wings and began to spill forth a stream of shrill nonsense.

"Down came a blackbird and snapped off her nose! Jack's no thief! Jack's no thief! The King of Tarts, *he* stole the hearts and sent them clean away! Clean away! Cleaning day! A clean sweep!"

And he turned his head and started to preen his feathers.

The Ring

NORA

I had searched the nursery often before, and now while Eelie slept I searched it again. There was really no likely place where Jack could have hidden my ring, but the despair was in me so that I could not sit still.

"Please, Jack," I begged the bird. "Please bring back my ring. If indeed you *are* changed, as the Erl Queen told me, then this is the time to be of service to me!"

The jackdaw cocked a malevolent eye at me and piped, "Four and twenty blackbirds were baked in a pie! But Jack's nobody's fool! Jack's nobody's fool!"

I tried flattery. "Dear Jack, I know you are wiser than all the other birds, wiser even than Raekkin and Grypyr. Come now, do help me find my ring!"

"Dunderheads! Blunderers!" Jack squawked.

Did he understand? Was he mocking me? "I've offered

you my gold coins, Jack," I said, "but all you ever did was take them away and hide them. What else can I offer you?"

"Sing a song of sixpence, fivepence, fourpence. I've got threepence, jolly jolly threepence. I've got threepence to last me all my life. Leg a derry, leg a merry! Mett, merr, whoop, whirl!" The bird danced up and down, screeching.

It was hopeless, but still I tried. "Jack, please help me, for no one else can. I cannot marry the Erl King!"

"Queen Nora!" the jackdaw said, and his small evil eye glittered like a shiny pearl bead in his coal-black head. "Queen Nora!" he said in a gloating voice. "Wasn't that a dainty dish to set before the King!"

I knew then that he understood. He laughed at me and enjoyed my trouble. He knew what I wanted, but he was too spiteful to help me.

The wind was blowing stronger, and the April sky was darkening with the coming of more rain. Jack would not help me. "What earthly use is it to argue with him?" I said aloud to myself.

"Clootie! Bring back Nana's ring!"

The small imperious voice made me start. I turned to see Prince Elver sitting up in the bed, his face flushed. Behind me I heard the flutter of wings and knew Jack was gone out the window. I ran to try to see where he flew, but already he was lost in the whirling cloud of birds that swirled through the sky. I turned to admonish the small Prince.

"You should not have called Clootie by his name," I said gently.

"Don't you know, Nana, I can call him by his name if I want to? Why didn't *you* call him by his *true* name? It's the only way to make him do what you want. Don't you know that?"

"I cannot call Clootie by name. Your mother the Erl

Queen made me promise not to, and even when I want to, I cannot seem to break that promise."

"I'm sorry she did that," Eelie said. "But *I'll* make him do anything you want. I wish it were all as easy as that." He gave a small sob. "I'm so sleepy now. . . ." And he turned away and curled up and fell asleep again almost at once.

I leaned over him and tucked the covers in around him, gazing at the delicate sleeping profile—the damp tousled hair, the closed eye fringed with dark lashes brushing the soft flushed cheek, the gently curled lips—as he breathed in and out already deep in sleep. My heart ached with love of him, and I stood gazing at him despondently. I felt hopelessly trapped.

I picked up some mending I had left unfinished. I sat in a chair and tried to sew; sewing always seemed to bring me a sense of peace. The flutter of wings came again, but I did not look up. The shining golden ring dropped into my lap. I snatched it up and held it tight in my hand. Then joyfully, with a feeling of elation, of release from danger, I untied the bit of soiled ribbon still attached to it and slid the ring onto my finger.

"Thank you, Jack," I whispered.

And as I spoke, I knew that Clootie had returned. He was there in the room. I turned to confront him. He stood a little behind me in the dark shadow, as dark as ever himself in his clothes and looks. He stepped forward, his light gray eyes, cold and sharp, fastened on mine. It seemed the bitterest irony that Clootie should return now that Raekkin was gone.

"You *were* my jackdaw!" I exclaimed, certain of it now. I started to speak his name, but could not. I was at a loss. "Shall I call you Hjuki?" I asked doubtfully.

"Whatever you've a mind to. It's a small matter to me. Jack's as good a name as any."

"Then I'll thank you, Jack, for returning my ring," I said solemnly. "But tell me, were you always my jackdaw, even before I came here?"

Clootie did not answer. He walked across to the window and leaned there looking out, his shoulders hunched up and his dark head cocked to one side—there was even the gray patch on the back of his head—so much like my bird that I wondered that I had ever doubted.

Outside, the rain began to fall, and I rose to close the casements. Clootie turned to look at me.

"So you want answers, do you? You've no power over me, Princess Nora. Why should I be prattling a lot of tittle-tattle to please you?"

"I never intended to turn you into a jackdaw," I said. "You were a jackdaw before ever I came here, and that was none of my doing, but I suppose someone must have been the cause of it."

He laughed—not just his spiteful laugh, a real laugh—and the old mischievous gleam came into his eyes. "A regular Nosy Nan you are! A Polly Pry! So you'd like to know the wherefores and the whys! Not very wise. But you know the part, why not the whole?" He paused and grinned gleefully. "It was Bab Magga made me a jackdaw the first go-around. She cast the spell that called up a go-between—a messenger —between this world and yours. The Erl Queen chose me to be the messenger and sent me over the sea to Bab Magga. I went in the shape of a jackdaw. Bab Magga put me in a cage and into the hands of your husband so I might be a spy in your household."

"Bab Magga." I repeated the name, trying to remember. I had known a Bab Magga in my old life. She lived in our village, but she was nobody I would ever talk to. "Why would she want you to spy on us?" I asked.

Clootie shrugged. "She's a witch of sorts. More a bitch

than a witch. She was bitter as wormwood and worm-eaten with jealousy. It was you she was jealous of. She wanted your husband for herself. That's what she had her fool's heart set on, but all her spells couldn't drag him away from you. They were weak spells and only half learned. I could have helped her, but I didn't—not until my Queen's need met Bab Magga's."

Clootie paused and looked at me with his old deliberate scorn. "All worlds intertwine, Princess Nora, and all needs meet somewhere in Time. If you had listened to some of what Raekkin's been teaching the Prince, you'd be wiser, and I'd not have to tell you this. Bab Magga's need and Queen Elva's need met, and that was a time of trouble here in Erland, when our Queen fell ill at the birthing of the Prince. Seven days she lay in labor, and even Raekkin could not help. Only the sorceress Groa could bring her babe alive into this world. Ah, then our Queen needed you, Princess Nora! She needed a king's daughter to nurse the babe, for she could not. It was then I *blew the dark horn,* and by that same *horn-blowing,* Bab Magga got her wish. Your husband and child are hers now. He married her!"

I felt that Clootie took malicious pleasure in telling me this! I did not know whether to believe him or not, but something in his grin convinced me that it was all true.

"No witch can take my husband and child for her own!" I cried. "Eben is my husband, and I am his wife. Even if he were to marry again, thinking me dead, even so he'll be mine again when I return home, for he loves me, as I love him!"

"So an extra marriage or two doesn't matter, eh, my lady? It would seem you've been making a great pother and collieshangie over nothing! If it makes no difference, why not agree at once to marry the King and save yourself a deal of dule and dree?"

"I have my ring," I said. "And it's as bright as new. The Erl King cannot expect me to marry him now."

Clootie laughed, his old rusty-hinge laugh. "You don't know our King," he said, "if you think as small a thing as a ring will stand in his way! It'll make no difference, I promise you. And now I'll go see about my dinner—and yours —since I'm steward again."

The Locked Door

EELIE

Clootie had told Nana the ring would make no difference, and Clootie was right. Nana had left the nursery to confront the Erl King with her gold ring bright on her finger. She returned and her ring was gone.

She came to me, her face white and drawn with anger and despair. "He took the ring from me," she told me. "He tore it off my finger and flung it in the lake. 'Maybe the fishes will bring it back to you,' he said! It's nothing but a game to him, and how can I win? He says we are to be married as soon as the guests can be invited. Oh, Eelie, I cannot bear it!" She sank into a chair and buried her face deep in her hands. Her long black hair fell sadly around her.

I felt sick inside. Nana's grief and fear were so much my own that I could not comfort her. Comfort was useless unless I could find some way to help her. *I am The Helper!*

I thought, but the words seemed lifeless; there was no fire in them. I felt weak and useless. I *must* be able to help her, I thought. I drew back into myself, testing all the possible uses of my Power, but none seemed useful. There was so much I did not know. I had studied and studied, but Raekkin had said it was a long learning, and I was only at the beginning. The knowledge I needed now was still unlearned. I even considered the matter of the fishes—having them find the ring. But finding the ring was pointless—I knew that much. The Erl King would play that game only as long as it amused him; then he would see to it that the ring vanished forever.

"You will have to escape," I said aloud. "You will have to escape from Ellorgore. But I don't know how. If Raekkin were here, he'd know what to do."

Nana raised her head. "If I could escape, I would," she said in a strange, lost voice. "I'm ready to do something desperate . . . anything!"

"We will have to get Clootie to help us," I said.

"Clootie!" Nana exclaimed. "Clootie would never help me. Never in this world! He hates me, I know it. He brought back the ring only because you ordered him to."

"That's right, Nana. I ordered him to! If I call Clootie by his true name, he *has* to do whatever I order him to do!"

"What is it you intend to order me to do, Prince Elver?" It was Clootie, standing there in the doorway. Clad in black, he was like a dark shadow against the door frame.

"Come in and shut the door!" I ordered.

Clootie came in and closed the door behind him.

I considered carefully just how to put it, then I took a deep breath. "Clootie! I command you to help Princess Nora escape from this castle before the Erl King marries her!"

"Very formal, very comprehensive!" Clootie said. There

was no warmth in Clootie, no trace of friendliness. His nature was twisted awry. But I did not feel the hatred that Nana felt. His pale eyes were winter cold, but still he spoke to me with exaggerated politeness. "I have been thinking, Your Highness. I have been thinking, myself, that it would not suit me to have Princess Nora be Queen of Erland. But how am I to fulfill Your Highness's royal command?"

"How should I know!" I said shortly. "You brought Nana here; you can take her back the same way!"

"A sending is not a calling," Clootie said. "Going and returning are by different roads, as you know."

Clootie had his old scheming jackdaw look about him now. He stood there, and it was as if he were considering whether to obey me or not. I waited and did not press him. At last Clootie said, "I know one who can help you—the Harper. He is an outlander too. I am sure he would be glad to help Princess Nora away from here, if it was to his advantage."

The Harper. I knew who it was that Clootie meant. The Harper was a wanderer through all lands.

"Is the Harper here?" Nana asked. "I thought he had gone."

"He has come back," Clootie said.

"How can he be of help?" I asked.

"He can harp the whole castle to sleep if he so chooses," Clootie answered.

That seemed hopeful. "But can he harp the King to sleep? That's not so easy. It's not easy to trick a Master of Magic. And how can we be sure he won't betray us to my father?"

Clootie smiled. "The Harper has harped the King to sleep before. He has no loyalty to the Erl King, and, what's more, he has been secretly in love with Queen Elva all these years. Now he has returned to Ellorgore and has found the

Queen dead. What's to keep him here? He would be glad to do the King a disservice. You offered your gold to me, Princess Nora. If you were to offer the same to the Harper, I feel sure he would be more than willing to take you away from here."

"Bring the Harper here then," I said. "Nana never did want that gold, did you, Nana?"

"No, Eelie. I will give it to him gladly," she said.

But Clootie looked at me appraisingly and then shook his head. "I do not think it would be wise to bring him here, Your Highness. It might arouse suspicion. I think it would be better if I arranged it."

"Very well, arrange it then!" I said grandly.

The Harper would help. That was what Clootie told us when he returned later that afternoon.

"He will help Princess Nora escape from the castle, and he'll lead her to the sea. All the Harper wants is the gold and two of the best horses in the stable."

"What he wants, he can have," I said. "I can't *give* him any horses, but if he can harp the guards to sleep, he can take all the horses he wants."

"He only wants two—two good ones," Clootie said.

"When can we leave?" Nana asked.

"It will have to be tonight," Clootie answered. "It may be your last chance. I'll come for you sometime tonight, whenever the way is clear."

"Can we trust Clootie?" Nana asked when he was gone.

"He *has* to do what I've ordered. I used his *true* name," I said, and added, "Don't worry, Nana."

But I myself worried. I lay awake that night worrying. It was such a simple plan, and simple plans are best. What could go wrong? But still I worried. I had to be sure that Nana would reach home safely. Letting Nana go was the hardest thing I had ever done in my life. But I had to do it. I couldn't let her be so unhappy.

And then a really dismaying thought struck me. Nana had made a promise to my mother, and a promise to the Erl Queen could not be broken. *Nana could not leave until I was able to walk alone!*

My mind whirled sickeningly. All my hopes of helping her escape were worthless. I tried to think what to do. The sheer impossibility of my being able to walk in time to help Nana overwhelmed me. I knew I *couldn't* walk . . . but *why* not? There must be a reason. Was it a spell laid on me? Raekkin had said I would walk someday. He had said, "Only you yourself can open the way."

Someone else had said almost the same thing . . . the words came to me, a hoarse muffled voice saying, "Only your own hand will unlock the door!" My mind rushed backward in time. I saw myself as a baby sitting on the square-topped stone on the tower top and, flanking me, the two great black ravens of Odin: Thought and Memory—Hugin and Munin! It was Munin who had spoken those words.

It was then I knew what blocked my way. He had locked the door for me on my earliest memories. *Something was hidden there that I must face.*

Now, at last, I turned inward into the night of my own mind, seeking the answer. Step by step I forced myself to walk that unseen path. It led deeper and deeper into blackness, until at last I stood shuddering at the door of my most secret fear. I could put out my hand and touch that door, solid and smooth and black, endlessly black, invisible until I touched it. Once before I had opened the door, but only a crack. I knew that hunger was behind that door, a hunger so grim that only a brief glimpse of it had completely terrified me. I remembered the winter wood on Owen's island. I had crouched there in the snow appealing to Hugin for help, and he had helped me.

Could I open that door again? What else was waiting within? I wanted to turn back, to flee in sheer terror back the way I had come! But I did not flee. Again I crouched, trembling. This time I appealed to Munin. "Munin," I whispered, "I need to remember. Help me remember!" And once more a black wingtip gently brushed my mind.

Under my hand the door swung slowly open. And waiting within was not only hunger but death, death stark and hideous, the death I had fought against so desperately from the moment of my birth.

I had waged that struggle for days, each day a gnawing terror of hunger. My Queen mother, near to dying herself, had had no milk for me. I had fought all alone—I a new-born babe, starving and shriveling, withering like a dried leaf, weakening hour by hour until I was only a shell, a dried, near-empty husk, barely holding the spark of life. I had willed myself to survive, and it had taken all the strength of my small lonely soul. It was Nana who had saved me, who had come from afar to take me to her breast and nourish me, *and never would I give her up, for losing her meant dying.*

But now when I faced it, I realized that it was a dead horror. I looked at it and finally understood how and why this hidden fear had crippled me all my short life. Now, at long last, this primeval fear had no power over me. I had new troubles, new problems to solve; new and perhaps equally grim struggles lay ahead.

I closed the door of memory again, gently, firmly. It was gone. I was free of the spell it had laid on me. "Thank you, Munin," I said softly.

And the dark feathery voice answered, "Walk bravely, Prince of Erland. Look ahead to the road you must tread, to the life you must lead. There is no turning aside."

I sat up and swung my legs over the side of the bed. Slowly I got to my feet and stood alone. With complete confidence, certain now that my legs would not fail me, I took the first steps I had ever taken alone in Erland.

The Harper

NORA

It had been before I regained my memory and my speech that the Harper had first come to the castle. Halevyn was the Harper's name. He did not sing of battles or heroes, not when he sang in Queen Elva's bower, where I came with the other ladies to listen to his harp, all of us close together, I with the baby Prince in my arms, all sitting quiet in the darkness about the Queen's bed, and only the glow of firelight in the room. I had never seen any man other than the King in the Queen's chambers. But that night the King was away on the hunt, and the Queen too ill to leave her bed. She would hear the Harper's songs, and so we all gathered to bear her company.

I for one was moved to tears by the sound of the harp—it seemed the sweetest music I had ever heard. Songs he sang made my heart shiver, so that I felt it would shatter like frail crystal. The Harper himself was handsome, but more than handsome. He had a strange intense face, long golden hair and beard, and compelling eyes that caught the firelight and glowed—and such a marvelous deep voice, resonant and booming as a trumpet or soft and light as bird song. His hands moving on the strings of the harp seemed to be plucking the music out of air.

In the darkened room it was almost as if the figures on the tapestries moved in step to his playing, and all around us, as we sat spellbound, a magic circle of dancers wove in and out through the flowering walls. But we were scarce aware, for our eyes were all on the Harper, and I was not the only one who sighed in the darkness as he sang:

> *If I sing sweeter than other minstrels*
> *It is because I have known your love.*
> *Here in this foreign land each thought of you*
> *Is as a flight of birds across the sky*
> > *through fire-flowing clouds.*
> *Ah, that my feet might follow where those birds fly.*

His voice and the notes wavered and swept up and down like birds' wings, fading away as the song ended.

I could gladly have listened all night to his playing, and indeed, it was nearly dawn, the first glimmer of pale light at the window, when at last he said that he was too weary to play more. Just one last song for farewell, the Queen asked, and he sang it—the saddest, sweetest song of all:

> *There are sharks that swim in the Seas of Evening, darling,*
> *So when you come to those moon-white waters pause,*
> *And there will come the Ship of the Sweet Star's Singing*
> *With silent oars*
> *To carry you across.*

> *There are quicksands on the Strands of Evening, darling,*

So do not try to cross that shining sand,
But wait until they beach their boats and cease their singing
And oars in hand,
Come to where you stand.

But now, my love, I cannot sing for weeping,
As ever in the darkling day
I hear the fluted barges round me ringing,
And you are lost
So far . . . so far away.

That was the last song Halevyn had sung, and its words and music had haunted my days and nights long after. It was as if he had let fall a line deep into my well of lost memory, and somewhere down in those depths a sliver of memory tugged like a fish at the end of a line. I would sing the song to myself, silently, for in those days I could not sing aloud. But in my thoughts it was Halevyn's voice I heard singing, and when I would come to those final words: "And you are lost so far . . . so far away," the tears would burn in my eyes. It was my husband and my child I had lost, but, try as I might, I could not pull that thought up to the surface of my mind.

Now as I remembered that night, I realized why I had felt that intense sorrow and longing, and the Harper's song meant more to me now that I knew why it had moved me so.

The Harper had left the castle soon after. If he had now returned and would help me to escape, what better hope did I have? I could not remain here any longer.

But it almost broke my heart to part from Eelie. And just at this moment, too, when he could walk at last. I longed to stay and share that triumph with him. He tried to tell me how it had come about—a spell lifted, a strange secret revealed by a black raven—but it was beyond me to understand his words. I cared little as to how it had come about. To me it was like a miracle, and I gave thanks for that. It seemed the best of omens. I could leave now more at ease in my mind, but still I wept at the parting.

"Please come with me, Eelie," I begged. But he would not.

"I cannot go with you, Nana," he said. His blue eyes grew solemn and filled with mystery. "I am the Erl Prince and this is my land. I must stay here."

That night I sat waiting, wrapped in my fur-lined mantle, with Eelie held tight in my arms, until we heard the first faint rippling notes of the harp, and Eelie said, "We mustn't listen, Nana. We must stop our ears." It was strange to sit there hearing nothing, keeping the sounds at bay, locked in dead silence as the black hours passed.

It was in the very small hours of the night, just as the dark was almost lightening, that Clootie came to fetch me. Outside our door the guards were slumped in sleep, and the great gray dog whimpering and growling as well in his dream-hunting. Even though he was asleep, I skirted him with care. And all the guards we passed, all were sunk in deep sleep.

I found Halevyn in the stable courtyard, dressed in chain mail, armed and helmeted. He had two horses saddled and ready. One was the great white horse Ornhest, the King's horse. And the other was a gray called Greyfrey. The two were surely the best in the King's stable! How could Halevyn be so rash as to steal the King's own horse? But then I realized that he was stealing the King's bride as well—myself —and what was a horse to that?

"You are in good time," Halevyn said. "The sooner we are out of here, the better."

"How long will the guards be sleeping?" I asked as I handed him my purse of gold coins.

He put it away in one of Ornhest's saddlebags. "It was a long harping," he said. "They will sleep fast until cockcrow." And he lifted me onto the gray's back.

Cockcrow! That seemed all too soon to me.

We rode out through the East Gate, a small gate that opened on a road leading down to the water. The sky was a chill steel-blue touched with the first faint tinge of dawn and with only a last few stars scattered here and there far apart. I thought we would be leaving by barge, but instead Halevyn rode the white horse directly into the lake. I hesitated, reining up the gray. I watched Halevyn ride straight out into the water; then he turned and waved to me to come ahead. I followed doubtfully, but the water was no deeper than to our horses' hocks. Looking down into the clear amber water, I could see what seemed like a stone causeway underfoot. It was an underwater road between the castle and the shore. We rode straight out into the lake for a way, and then Halevyn pulled up the white horse and waited until I caught up with him.

"The Water Road changes direction here," he said. "Follow close on my heels or you'll be in over your head!"

He did not smile. He had a rather grim air about him. It was a long water journey across the dark lake, with a chill wind blowing, and several times we made odd changes of direction. I was glad of the darkness, but gladder that I had Halevyn for a guide.

"When was this road built?" I asked him.

"Long ago, before they built the castle. They planned it so, to protect the castle from invaders."

I looked back at Castle Ellorgore, now far behind us, its battlements black against the cloud-streaked western sky, and suddenly my remorse at leaving Eelie swept over me again, and the tears came. I was weeping openly when at last we came out onto the far shore where a lacy fringe of winter ice was still clinging.

"Why all the tears?" Halevyn asked. "You're through safely so far."

"It's not that," I said. "It's not that I'm afraid. It's leaving my baby, my Prince. I can't help but weep when I think of him."

"You could have your babe and his father too!" Halevyn said. "If you want to return, you had better tell me. I'm taking more risk than I care for. If you're going to have a change of heart, I would as soon send you back right now!"

"No," I said. "No, I have to leave. I cannot marry the Erl King."

"Too ugly for you?" Halevyn asked lightly.

"I'm married already," I said.

"If you weren't married, would you have him? You would be Queen and the Prince your son."

"No," I said. "Nothing could make me marry him!"

"Then let us go!" Halevyn said. He put spurs to the white horse. Ornhest surged forward in a great bound and galloped off down the forest track.

I followed and we rode at full speed and no stopping. All I remember is a cold wind whistling about us, the thudding of hoofs, the earth rushing away below, and the blur of pale green leaves. There was no open country, only deep woodland, shadowy and wild. Halevyn spoke no word and never looked back. We both knew that the King's men would be coming in pursuit. Even now they might have discovered our flight. So we rode as if they were close on us. The white horse's flanks rippled like white water, his mane and his long tail streaming like spray in a tempest, and my gray horse pounded steadily behind. Greyfrey was no match for Ornhest, but he was a fine strong horse and swifter than any I had ever ridden.

As we traveled ever deeper into the forests of Erland, the

ground grew steadily rougher, with steep mounting hills and deep fern-filled glens, so that we were forced to go more slowly. The trail branched often, and Halevyn seemed always to choose the narrowest and least traveled of the ways. I was glad of the slower pace, for the gray was winded, and I doubted if otherwise he could have kept up with Ornhest.

I was growing weary, too, and saddle-sore as the day wore on, for it was long since I had ridden a horse. In all those years I had never left the castle. Now I felt like a freed prisoner, here in this lost wild forest among the towering tree trunks, where the first pale leaves of spring glowed shimmering against the darkness. Thick in among the delicate greens and pinks stood the ancient green-black conifers with the wind blowing great showers of needles down from their tall tops.

As we rode along, six snow-white doves flew by and settled in a hazel bush ahead of us.

Flight

EELIE

It was a sad, tearful parting with Nana. I hated that. And I hated it when she was gone with Clootie and I was left all alone in the great empty room. I felt so lost and lonely that I wished I had gone with her. But I couldn't go. I was the Erl Prince and this was my land. I had to stay here.

I looked at the moon cupboard, and I felt better just thinking about visiting her and Owen in Midgard. But still I was miserable, knowing that she would not be here with me any more. The room was so empty now that she was gone.

Suddenly the thought came to me: *I don't have to sit here alone; I can go see Nana leaving!* Not to the stable courtyard —that might cause trouble. But I would be able to see her if I climbed the Southeast Tower. There was nothing to stop me. I jumped up and ran out and up the stairs to the battlements and crossed over to the tower. There were some guards about, but they all seemed as if they were sleepwalking. If they were surprised to see me out there walking around in the early-dawn darkness, none of them tried to interfere with me.

I climbed the tower stairs and came out on the crenellated top. My legs were really tired by the time I climbed all those stairs. I was afraid I would miss seeing Nana go, but when I looked out I could still see them, just barely—a white horse and a gray horse far out in the middle of the lake. They were following the underwater road. If you hadn't known they were horses, you would have thought them just a pair of gulls way out there, for the gray horse was almost invisible against the dark lake water. I shaded my eyes and squinted, trying to see more clearly. Then I climbed on top of one of the merlons. It was still so dark and so far away and I was so high up that I couldn't really be sure that it was Nana. I wished I could see them better. I leaned out as far as I could, straining to see.

Suddenly—without thought, without meaning to—I had launched myself into the air! I fell, floundering desperately, flailing my arms and legs and feeling the air rushing past. Down, down I plunged, at terrifying, sickening speed. Then I caught myself and spread my wings. I could see the great bronze pinions unfurl on either side. They swept through the air in great powerful strokes, carrying me effortlessly. I did not need to learn to fly—I was flying! It was as simple as that.

I was flying, as if this were the only right way to move. The shape I was in was the shape of a great golden eagle, not a fledgling eagle, but a full-grown eagle in the proudness of his full strength—and I knew that this was my true and natural form. It was as if I had come into my rightful heritage, into a world that was truly my own, the Sky World of air and wind and clouds. I was my *true* self at last, a being of the sky, as light as an armful of air, designed to soar and glide in perfect freedom, to dive down at will, plummeting toward the earth, to rise to the sun—to ride the air currents high, high above the land so infinitely far below.

Off to the east I could see the red disk of the sun just rising out of the sea. I could see the dark forests and silver lakes of Erland spread out below me. My eagle eyes were so sharp that I could count every leaf on a tree and every hair in Ornhest's mane and tail. I could see every smallest detail as Nana and the Harper galloped swiftly into the forest. It was Ornhest that the Harper rode. How could he have dared to take the King's own horse! I wondered at that.

I was watching, too, from high in the sky, as a troop of soldiers rode out the East Gate in pursuit. They rode splashing through the water, and two slipped off the Water Road and were left behind floundering in the lake. I sailed high above and saw more troops come pouring out of the castle like tiny ants swarming out of an anthill.

But by then Nana and Halevyn had left the main trail far behind and were traveling far to the east through the low wooded hills. I watched through the day, soaring high overhead, as they traveled in a wide circle toward the north. The soldiers pursued them, charging off in many directions, but always far, far behind the two fugitives. It was like a play, far away and remote, and yet I was there, too, so close to Nana that I could see the tearstains on her cheeks. My farseeing eyes could pick out every tiniest detail, but my ears could not hear what was being said down there, so far below.

I turned my eyes on the Harper. There was something about him, something not quite right. He was something other than he seemed to be. I could not quite bring him into focus, although I could see every feature of his handsome face, each hair in the golden beard as it curled and twisted in and out. Ornhest tossed his head and the white flecks of foam from his bit flew backward, spattering the rider. Halevyn put out his hand and patted the great curved white neck.

A shudder went through me, out to the tips of my great wings. Now I knew why Clootie had not wanted me to meet the Harper! *He knew I would know who and what he was.*

But what I did not know was how I could save Nana now.

The Doves

NORA

The six white doves were still sitting in the hazel bush as we rode by. Their thick throaty cooing filled the air, and in the soft sounds they made I could hear words:

> *Be not beguiled, fair one, fair one.*
> *The false knight is beguiling thee.*
> *We are six lost ones, lost ones,*
> *And thou shalt be the seventh.*

"Be still, you silly jills!" Halevyn shouted, and the doves took flight.

"What did they mean?" I asked, for I could not be certain I had really heard those strange words.

"It is an old song, the dove's song," he said. "No one heeds the foolish birds."

The six doves flew ahead of our horses and settled again in a small tree. Their cooing lament sounded even more ominous, for now I felt sure I heard my name and Halevyn's:

> *Be not beguiled, Nora, Nora!*
> *Be not beguiled by his fair form.*
> *Let him go in beast's shape;*
> *The wolf is no bloodier killer!*
> *Be not beguiled, Nora, Nora!*
> *Halevyn is beguiling thee.*

A chill like frost touched my heart. I glanced at Halevyn doubtfully. Was I only imagining that I had heard those words?

"What a sad sound the doves make," I said.

"Doves are always complaining," Halevyn said. "They complain that their feet are pink because they must walk barefoot through the winter's frost and snow." And he laughed.

But I did not feel like laughing with him. I think he sensed my uneasiness, for I saw his face grow hard, and a coldness came into his eyes.

We rode on through the dark-barred woodland, and no other word was spoken between us. At last, as the afternoon wore on and the shadows grew deeper and longer, I begged him to stop so that we might eat.

"We will find meat soon," Halevyn said, and he rode on.

Only a little way more, and I saw ahead of us strange shapes hanging in a great oak. I saw that they were three hanged men dangling there. About them hovered a flock of black carrion birds; some perched on the sun-blackened corpses and tore at the rotted stinking flesh. My stomach revolted at the sight, and I turned my head away as we drew nearer the gallows tree.

Halevyn reined up beneath the wide death-bearing branches and, looking up, laughed aloud. "Here's meat for you!" he said.

I shuddered and urged my horse on. Halevyn followed, still chuckling at his grim joke. "I thought you were hungry, my lady!"

"What kind of jest is that?" I cried in anger. "I would rather die than eat such flesh!"

"You would do better to feed as the carrion birds feed," Halevyn said, "for you will never eat bread again."

I said nothing. I could not understand this black mood that was on him. It seemed he, too, had understood the doves' words and was angered at me for heeding them.

I tried to keep silent, but I felt so sick at heart and so faint that at last I said, "Cannot we stop to drink?"

"The moss water is unwholesome," he said. "A little way, and we will find wine."

We rode until he reined up beside a spring. "Here's a spring that flows wine," he said. "Here you may drink."

But I stared at the spring with horror, for it was not water or wine that flowed from it, but red blood!

"I cannot drink from such a spring," I whispered. "I would sooner die!"

"If you are thirsty, drink!" he said harshly. "For you will never drink wine again!"

Cold fear flowed into the hollow of my heart, but what could I do but follow where Halevyn led? Deeper and deeper into the dark woods we rode, deep into the shadow world of trees. Halevyn looked back over his shoulder and must have seen the white look on my face. He smiled at me then, his quick charming smile, and spoke kindly. "There's no need to fear, Princess Nora. Soon we will reach a fair haven. At Wearie's Well our horses may drink, and there we will find sweet rest."

His strange, frightening mood seemed to have passed. Indeed, he unslung his harp and played a gay tune as we rode along, and he sang:

Look away! Look away
Over Yandro's high hill
Where those little white doves are a-flyin'
From bough to bough
And a-mating with their mates.
And why not I with mine,
Oh sweet my love,
And why not I with mine?

But though his singing was cheerful, it failed to hearten me. His sudden changes of mood only made me more uneasy. Had Clootie known what sort of man he was? It would be like Clootie to send me forth with a guide who could not be trusted.

The sun sank slowly below the treetops and glinted red through the branches. We came at last to an open glade deep with greenness, the mossy ground scattered with toadstools of all hues. Like flowers they seemed in the green glade, all their strange colors glowing in the rose-gold light of evening. In the center of the glade was a great wide pool, the water still and black, smooth as a sheet of black glass. An eerie silence hung over the place, and no birds sang in the trees.

I was so weary by then that I wanted only to rest, and I was glad when Halevyn stopped his horse and dismounted. He courteously lifted me down from my saddle, but as he set my feet on the ground, he clasped me tighter in his arms.

"Come now, give me a kiss," he said, "for I have brought you safe to Wearie's Well. Here we will sleep, and before we sleep we shall be lovers and have much delight in each other."

But I pulled away from him and shook my head. "No," I said. "Oh, no!"

"It was part of the bargain, Nora," he said. "You cannot refuse me my payment for aiding you to escape from the Erl King!"

"It was no part of the bargain," I answered. "I promised you my gold, and that I gave you gladly, but I will not be your lover, or your mistress, or your wife, for I have a husband already—but do not be offended, Halevyn," I added, for I saw his face darkening. "That is the same answer that I gave to the Erl King."

I could see the fixed black anger in his eyes, and his voice was no longer gentle. The words were terrible that he spoke.

"The devil consume you and all virtuous maidens! There is the mouth of Hell!" He pointed to the black pool. "I have drowned six kings' daughters in that pool, and you shall be the seventh! Am I as ugly as the Erl King that you should spurn me?"

He was not ugly to look at, but I was horror-struck by his words.

"The doves warned you, didn't they, Nora? The six white doves—the souls of the six maidens I drowned. It would have been better for you if you had not listened to them! I give you the same choice I gave the others: come to me, or go to your death!"

I looked at the pool. It seemed both wide and deep, with a black deadliness about it, but it did not frighten me as much as Halevyn did.

"I will go to my death rather than to you," I said and took a step toward the water's edge.

But he reached out and seized my arm. His voice was harsh. "Take off that golden gown! Take off your finery!" he ordered. "It is not fitting that such rich goods should rot in the waters of Wearie's Well!"

I took off my gown and my shift, as he ordered, and the gold combs binding my hair, and naked I walked to the brink. I drew a deep breath and I dived deep into the pool.

Down I went, down through water as black as ink, and not a handsbreadth could I see before my face. Down I plunged deep into the icy depths and turned swooping upward again, my hair sweeping about me. I felt my hands touch the smooth trunk of a submerged tree. I held it briefly with both hands and was about to thrust away from it and swim clear when suddenly there, deep in the water, the tree trunk moved and slid smoothly between my hands, and I felt the cold deadly life in it. Then against my bare thighs I felt another thick coil sliding, closing about me. In sheer stark horror I kicked free and shot up to the surface, breaking through with a terrified scream.

"Help me!" I screamed in uncontrolled terror. "Eelie! Eelie! *Hjälper, save me!*" I was past knowing what I cried. But I saw Halevyn leaning over the water, and suddenly anything seemed better than the black horror below. "Halevyn, pull me out!" I pleaded. "I'll do anything! I promise! Anything you ask!"

Halevyn leaned nearer and stretched out his hand. "Is it so? Then catch hold of my hand!"

I reached desperately for his hand, and he drew me close to the edge, but he did not pull me up. "Kiss me then, Nora," he said. "Kiss me to seal the bargain."

He drew me partly out of the water. As he knelt at the edge, my other hand reached up to clutch at his collar, and our lips met. My eyes were fastened on his fair face, and I felt it was no ill bargain—better far to live and be loved by such a knight than be dragged down by the water monster's coils into that black hole of Hell.

But as our lips met and I felt his mouth pressed against mine, his face seemed to blur, to melt and change, and it was no longer Halevyn that I clutched so desperately. It was the ugly, ogrelike face of the Erl King that pressed his lips

193

to mine, and the hand that held my hand was a repulsive knobbed and warty thing. I screamed and flung myself backward into the pool. I was still clutching the Erl King's collar, and I dragged him in after me. Then we were both floundering together in the water.

I saw and felt the great gleaming coils of the water monster writhing about us, entwining themselves about the body of the Erl King, and I heard the dreadful screech of fury that tore from his throat. I was free of his hands and swimming frantically for safety. I managed to reach the pool's edge. I flung myself bodily out of the water, snatching at the grasses that overhung the steep brink, and clawed my way up until I found myself, panting and dripping, naked on solid ground. I turned then and looked behind me and saw the water of the pool churning as the Erl King was dragged under. But he rose again, screaming curses at me.

"You false bitch! You gave me your word!"

I shivered, unable to answer, but a small child's voice answered for me. "She said she'd be yours if you pulled her out! But she pulled herself out—and you in! Lie there in that black hole with the six maidens you've murdered and keep them company!"

"I should have killed you, too, you damned brat!" the King roared. He tried to heave himself out of the water, but he sank back and was pulled under, and once more his head vanished below the surface. The water closed over him and he did not reappear. Slowly the ripples spread wider and wider, and then the pool was as still and glasslike as before. I turned to see my small Prince standing beside me.

"You were right, Nana," he said. "We should not have trusted Clootie. But I'll punish him. Please don't cry, Nana."

For I was weeping as I knelt beside him. "Oh, Eelie,"

I cried, "forgive me! It's your father I've drowned!"

"He was an evil man, Nana!" Eelie said, and his eyes looked fierce as he frowned at me. "It was evil to try to kill you. You didn't drown him, it was the water monster did that. I'm glad you called me, but I think you should get dressed now. It's cold here."

The sun had entirely set, only the twilight lingering in that eerie glade, and I was shivering. "We can't stay here," I said as I dressed.

"I'll take you away," Eelie said seriously, "and I'll stay with you, so nothing can hurt you. Will you please help me on your horse, Nana? It's too tall for me."

I laughed through my tears as I lifted him, so small, onto Greyfrey's saddle. I laughed to think that one who had such magical powers, one who could come from far away to save me from death—that such a one should be too small and weak to climb on the back of a horse.

I took the white horse's reins and tied them to my gray horse's graithing. Then I climbed into the saddle behind my small Prince. I encircled him with my arms, and we left that unholy place behind.

The Flame Circle

EELIE

Nana's arms were tight around me as we rode away from that place. I could feel her still shivering. But right then I really wasn't thinking very clearly. I wasn't thinking about what I had done, and what it would mean. I was just glad that Nana was safe, and proud that I had been able to help her. Deep inside I had the warm, comforting feeling that now Nana wouldn't have to go away; now I could take her back with me to Ellorgore.

But the forest was darkening as the light faded, and I wasn't sure which way we were going. I knew Nana was exhausted, so I suggested that it was time to stop and rest.

We dismounted in a forest clearing, and she held the horses while I concentrated hard on making a fire—a Flame Circle of protection. I stood in one spot, my arms held out straight on both sides, reaching to the farthest limits of my

Power, and as I turned, a distant line of flame crept through the forest, gradually encircling us.

Nana gazed at the line of fire as it crept through the underbrush, and I realized that she was worried. "It's a Flame Circle," I said. "It's to keep the wild animals away. See, Nana, it's not going to burn the woods. It's just going to stay in a circle, the way it should."

Although she did not understand the magic of it, she was glad to be safe inside the circle. We took the bridles off the horses so they could graze, and Nana loosened the saddle girths, but we left them saddled. The circle was quite large. It was really beautiful, as beautiful as the rowan tree flames. All the tree shadows loomed dark beyond the ring of fire where we sat in the center. Just enough heat reached us so that it was comfortable. We found a flask of wine and also bread and cheese in Ornhest's saddlebags. The food made Nana feel better, and the wine gave her courage to tell me all about what had happened on the journey with Halevyn. She told me about the white doves and about the gallows tree and the spring that flowed blood. I knew that the tree and the spring were magic, but it was evil magic, and I was glad that the doves had tried to warn Nana.

Then we lay down to sleep. There were beasts' eyes glowing in the darkness beyond the Flame Circle, but I knew they would never step inside it. I slept warm and sound, folded close in Nana's arms with her fur-lined mantle wrapped around us both. I dreamed of flying, of soaring high over the trees. I was just swooping by over a great oak when I heard a terrible screaming.

I started up, wide-awake, and Nana grabbed tight hold of me as Ornhest came charging out of the night. Right up to us he came, snorting wildly. He turned and tossed his great head, and his mane swung up and down, flashing white in the darkness. He neighed loudly and stamped his hoofs. Another shrill scream came, shattering the night.

"What is it, Ornhest?" I gasped. Nana and I were both on our feet, staring into the outer dark. Ornhest was trembling and blowing great blasts from his nostrils. I suddenly realized that I could not see Greyfrey anywhere inside the circle of fire. It wasn't that I was brave, it was more that I was foolish, for I ran out at once toward the flames, shouting the gray horse's name. "Greyfrey! Greyfrey!"

Greyfrey was not there, but near the circle's edge I almost ran right into a great mess of blood. It was splashed all around, red and sticky on the green ferns and the forest floor, more blood than I had ever seen before. I could even smell the thick sickening smell of it. I knew it was Greyfrey's blood.

I stood staring at the blood, and out in the darkness beyond I heard snarlings and growlings and grisly crunchings of bones. Then suddenly the most awful howl—not a scream like before, but a high-pitched shrieking wail—made me jump in pure fright, and my hair stood up on me. In that moment of *uncontrolled* fear, I felt rather than heard the voice inside my head. It was an evil gloating voice. It said:

> First the gray horse,
> Then the white horse,
> Next the nurse,
> And last the little baby!

I knew then what it was, and I felt sick with the knowledge. It was a Spirit Beast mocking me . . . and *I knew what Spirit Beast it must be.*

All this happened in less than a minute. Then Nana was calling me and running toward me where I stood near the edge of the circle. I whirled and ran back to her, yelling, "Stay there, Nana! Stay there!"

She reached out and grabbed me, her eyes wide open with terror. "What is it?" she said. "What's out there?"

I was ashamed of myself for scaring her. "It's nothing, Nana! It's just the wind howling. It scared the horses. Greyfrey has run away. But we'll find him in the morning. Come on, Nana," I coaxed, "let's go back to sleep. We've got a long way to go tomorrow."

But although Nana fell asleep, it was because I sang her the rune song of sleep. I did not dare go to sleep myself. I stayed awake and on guard. Ornhest stayed close to us, and I felt his breath going in and out over my head like a bellows in a forge.

I had a lot to think about that night. I remembered things Raekkin had told me—how without a Departing through Fire the soul of a dead Shape Changer could not go free. It would come back in the form of beast or bird and roam through Erland until it killed the one who had caused its death.

So the white doves were the souls of the drowned princesses, and they had brought my father to his death. Now he too was a Spirit Beast—the beast out there beyond the Flame Circle, that was my father, the Erl King. And I knew now that Nana would never be safe in Erland. I could not take her back with me to Ellorgore. I would have to see that she got away safe over the sea to the other world—to Midgard —where the Spirit Beast could not follow.

Even if the Spirit Beast had not threatened her, I knew that it would not be right to keep Nana any longer in Erland. She had been held here too long already, and all this evil was the result. She was Owen's mother, not mine. He needed her. I smiled then, thinking of the two of them meeting at last in Midgard! And Eben too—I would have to free Eben from the spell. I thought about that. It might not be easy.

The spells of Erland were not easily broken.

That was not all I had to think about. I had to think about being King of Erland, because that's what I was—and what I had been from the moment the water monster had drowned my father in Wearie's Well.

I had never really *thought* about what it meant to be King. I had thought it was a long way off. It would not be easy. I knew I was too young, but there was no way I could *not* be King, for there was no one else to inherit the throne of Erland.

My father had been a powerful king, but he had been feared rather than loved. I had heard stories of how he had misused his Power. You had to be careful with Power; even your own Power could turn against you and destroy you. Power had made my father evil.

I knew the kind of king I wanted to be. I wanted to be powerful but wise. I had flown high over this land on eagle wings, over its silver lakes and dark forests, and I realized how vast a domain it was. It was a beautiful land, but it was more than lakes and forests—there were people as well, with all their troubles and sorrows and needs. I wanted to *help* the people of Erland. *I was The Helper!* That meant more to me than a crown or a throne.

I thought about this a long time, and I was glad that I would have Raekkin and Grypyr to advise me. There might be others beside Clootie who would try to betray me. I thought about loyalty and what it meant. Loyalty meant love. I loved Raekkin and Grypyr and they loved me. I would always be able to trust them completely. Nana had said that Clootie hated her. But I had felt no hatred in Clootie—no love either, only a sort of malice. I had tried to bind him with orders, orders he was forced to obey, but somehow it hadn't worked. Maybe such orders never would work.

There would always be a way to obey and yet betray at the same time.

I thought about these things until my head swam and my eyes wouldn't stay open. I don't know when I fell asleep, but I slept, and Ornhest stood guard over us.

Ornhest

EELIE

I awoke in the wet gray dawn, the trees all dripping with night mist, but around us the Flame Circle still burned. I awoke with the feeling of dread hanging over me, and the need to act. Ornhest whinnied as I scrambled to my feet. Nana was still sleeping, and I did not wake her up, not until I had got the bit in Ornhest's mouth and the bridle over his head, for I wanted to see if I could do it by myself. He seemed to want to help me; he lowered his head way down to the ground so I could reach, and he opened his mouth and took the bit himself. Then he pawed the earth as if to say, "Let's get going!"

I woke up Nana and we ate some breakfast while we waited for the sun to come up, so we would know where the east was. I knew the sea was to the northwest; I had seen it there when I was flying overhead.

"We'll have to ride Ornhest," I told Nana. "I can't find Greyfrey." I did not tell her that I had not looked for the gray. I did not need to look.

Nana considered the white horse doubtfully. "He's so big and strong," she said. "I don't know if I can control him. Grypyr always said no one could ride him but the King. I suppose—" She broke off and then went on. "I suppose I should have known that Halevyn was really King Elrik—because he rode Ornhest. But how could he look so different, Eelie? I don't understand how he could change his appearance like that."

"He was a Shape Changer," I said. "All kings of Erland are Shape Changers, and some others too—like Clootie. We are not all Shape Changers here in Erland, but all those of royal blood are. Ornhest will carry us, because *I'm* King of Erland now."

The sun was coming up now like white fire through the trees. So we mounted Ornhest. I let the Flame Circle die, and we rode off toward the northwest, toward the sea. What mattered was getting to the sea before dark. I was afraid that if we were forced to spend another night in the woods, my Flame Circle would not protect us any better than it had before, and the Spirit Beast would kill Ornhest, as he had threatened to. Then Nana and I would be left afoot in the forest, and he would get Nana, too, before we could reach the sea. Even reaching the sea would not help if we did not have Ornhest with us, or so I thought. I know now that there were many ways we might have traveled, but then it seemed that everything depended on Ornhest.

We rode as swiftly as we could, galloping down the forest tracks—some so narrow that they were like footpaths winding among the tall tree trunks. I kept calling, "Go faster, Ornhest! Take us to the sea!"

He seemed to understand, for he whinnied and tossed his head so that his mane frothed about us. Like a white wind in the trees, he swept through the forest. When I looked back over my shoulder, I could see a distant movement, a shadow ranging just beyond the edge of my sight. I could not see it clearly, but I knew it was there—always coming, steadily, grimly, on our trail.

I did not tell Nana we were being followed.

We did not stop to eat. We kept going all day. Ornhest's neck and shoulders were soaking wet with sweat, and the reins were white with lather, but he never slowed down. Finally, as the sun was dropping low in the sky, he let out a great triumphant neigh, and I knew we were nearing the sea at last. Soon I could smell a strange salty smell, and I saw the glint of water shining through the trees. The smell was different from the smell of lake water, and the sea, when we came out of the woods, was vaster than any lake. Endless water stretched away to the very edge of the earth, and I wondered that there could be another land way out there, a land that we could not see.

A rough pebbly stretch led down to the water, and the great waves came surging in, cresting and curling over, frothing white and crawling up the beach.

I was glad we had reached there before dark. But Nana just stared about us at the rocky shore with the wild forest spreading on both sides, and she said, "Where are the boats? How will we find a ship, Eelie?"

"You'll ride home on Ornhest," I told her. "He's a Water Strider. He'll carry you across the sea."

Nana turned to look at me and laughed, but it wasn't a happy laugh. "Eelie, I know you can make magic. But this is too much magic! Magic is mostly believing, and I can't believe that a *horse* can carry me across the ocean!"

"Well, he can," I said. "And believing has nothing to do with *real* magic. If you don't believe, it doesn't matter. He still can."

"I think perhaps I'd have the courage to try if you were with me, Eelie. Please come with me."

"I can't come with you, Nana. I wish I could. But I have to stay in Erland and be King. I have to. But you'll get there safely. If you're too scared, just close your eyes and don't look. Just keep your eyes closed until you get there."

Nana gazed at the great stretch of sea beyond the foaming breakers, the water gleaming deep lavender now as the sun sank down. A low fog bank far off was turning flame red, and a flight of seabirds flew across, far out there, black against the flowing red clouds.

"If I must do something that unbelievable," Nana said slowly, "I'd rather do it with my eyes open."

I knew then that she would be all right.

"There are some things I have to tell you, Nana, before you go. There are two things that you must not do. You must *never* touch the dark horn that hangs on Ornhest's saddle, and you must not go back to your house until you find Eben."

"But how can I find Eben if I don't go home to our house?" Nana asked.

I tried to be very careful in what I said. "You must listen to what I'm saying, and you must *remember*, for I can't explain it all now."

"All right, Eelie," she said. "Go on, I'll listen."

"Ornhest is going to take you over the sea. He'll take you to an island where you'll find Owen. You'll know Owen because you've seen him once, and he'll know you. But Eben may be there and he may not. You must wait on that island until Eben comes. Then Ornhest will take you all home. Owen will be afraid to go back, but tell him that I said it will be safe to go home. Can you remember all that?" I asked anxiously.

"I will remember," she said. "About the horn and Eben and Owen. But it's all so mixed up I know I'll never understand, so don't try to explain. I have understood very little of all that has happened since I came to this land."

"You don't have to understand," I said.

"I know. I don't even have to believe, but I do believe that you can make impossible things happen. I love you, Eelie, and always will."

"Nana," I said, "*I am Hjälper*. Remember that, too. If ever you need help again, call me and I'll come, over the sea and farther."

"Oh, Eelie," she whispered, and her eyes filled with tears. "Oh, Eelie, how can I say good-by again!"

"Don't cry," I said—though I felt like crying, too. "Don't cry. I'll come and see you, even if you don't need my help."

She laughed at that and hugged me tight. Then I slid off down to the ground from the horse's back. Ornhest lowered his head, and I put my hand on his bridle and whispered into his ear.

"Ornhest, I want you to carry Nana safe across the sea to Rowan Tree Island in Midgard. Stay with her until she is safe in her own home, and then come back to Ellorgore." Then I gave the signal—the Water Strider words, "*Støkk yfir vatn!*"

Ornhest pawed at the earth. I knew he understood, so I let him go. He sprang down the rocky beach toward the water. Nana looked back at me, her face white, but I waved cheerfully. Ornhest charged splashing through the churning milky froth at the tide's edge and leaped the first great inrushing wave as if it were a wall. His hoofs struck the water beyond with a sound like thunder, and he galloped right out across the surface as if he were on dry land. He swept across the lavender water like blowing sea foam, his white tail and mane and Nana's black hair streaming in the wind. Nana clung tight to the saddle and didn't look back again.

I watched them go far out across the water, the water turning purple in the distance, and the horse and rider getting smaller and smaller until they looked like one of the white crests of the waves—and then I could not see them at all.

The Spirit Beast

EELIE

I turned back into the dark wood and waited. I knew the pursuer would soon find me. I did not know in what shape he would come, but I knew I must face him. I was King of Erland now, and I could not flee from a dead king's ghost no matter in what grim shape it might come.

I waited under a great black fir as the evening sky changed to a deep blue-green. There was a hushed silence all about me. Even the wild wood fowl were silent. Not a breath stirred in the treetops.

And he came, moving swiftly through the trees. I saw the dark shape approaching, running silently close to the ground following our trail—a four-footed beast, running head down at first, and then, as he realized I was near, the great head came up, the pointed ears pricked forward, and he came swiftly, charging toward me out of the gloom. His eyes glowed like gold fire in the dark. A great grisly wolf shape, larger than I had expected. I felt fear running through me, an icy shivering in my blood, but I stood fast in that spot, and he stopped. We looked each other full in the eyes.

He pulled back his lips to show the great yellow fangs and glared at me with those evil firelike eyes. "Run!" he growled. "Run! Run if you can. You won't run far!"

"I can run, but I won't!" I said. "I am not going to run from a dead king. I am alive, and I am King of Erland now, and you are only a spirit wolf. You have no Power over me!"

"I'll show you what Power I have!" he snarled, and the gray guard hairs were all bristling along his back. "I have the Power to kill you here and now. I have the fangs to tear your throat open!"

I had known he would have Power, but I had not known that I would still be powerless against him. I realized this too late. But I remembered one thing in time—I remembered Grypyr's gift. I had a weapon to call on, and I cried the name aloud, *"Vegandi!"*

It sprang into my hand—a long blade quivering like fire. The great wolf stood stock-still. He did not retreat, but he did not move an inch forward. His eyes were fastened on mine, and his snarl was as fierce as ever, his teeth long and gleaming. And he growled from deep in his chest, a series of ferocious growls, ever louder and more threatening. He was trying to make me give way, trying to unnerve me, trying to force me to show weakness. It was terrifying to hear, but I did not back away. I took a step forward instead. I strode toward him and slashed at him with the sword. He jumped back, and then I knew he was more afraid than I was. The Spirit Slayer forced him back, and I made him retreat, step by step, for ten paces or so. Then I stopped and put the point of the sword into the ground. The dry fallen needles began to smoke and glow with flame where the blade touched the earth.

The great wolf glared at me. He had stopped snarling and growling. "Very well," he said slowly, menacingly. "Very well, small one. But remember this: I will not forgive or forget. You could have helped me, but instead you saved that bitch of a nurse of yours. You'll meet me again in many a nightmare on many a night. I'll follow you and kill you in your dreams over and over again, and no sword of flame will guard you or save you. I'm a Demon of Night now, and I'll not let you sleep in peace, not ever again!"

"You forget," I said. "You keep forgetting that I am King of Erland now. The white horse Ornhest is mine to ride in the Wild Hunt. If you come to me again, even in one nightmare, I'll hunt you through the dark and across the sky and beyond the End of Time. The Hounds of the Wind will harry you to the far ends of Erland, beyond Fire and Ice, and the black Demons of Flight will never let you rest!"

The wolf's ears were back, flattened on his head, and I saw the gold fire die in his eyes. But still he stared at me.

"Father," I said, more gently now, "what you did, you did, and I will forgive you. What I did, you will have to accept. It is better if we make peace. I must live and be King, or the Kingdom of Erland will die with me, for I have no son yet. I know I do not have my full Power, but I will grow and learn, and someday I will be as powerful a king as you were. If you want to help me acquire the knowledge of Power, I will be glad of your help. If you won't help me, at least leave me in peace, for I don't want to keep fighting you forever."

The wolf's dead glassy eyes stared at me, and then he spoke. "Yes," he said softly, "you are King now. You are worthy to be called my son. I'll accept that."

I let my sword die away. The flame went gray and cold

and crumbled into ashes. I walked slowly forward, holding out my hand, and the great wolf waited quietly as I approached. His ears were still flattened back, and his tail drooped. I touched his head and slowly stroked it. The tip of his tail moved slowly, a faint back-and-forth motion, and then I was surprised, for his tongue flicked out and licked my face! Just that one brief kiss, and he turned and leaped away into the deep forest night.

I stood there with my heart pounding, shivering now with relief, and with a mixed-up feeling of joy and age-old sorrow.

I stared at the black forest wall where he had vanished. Only the darker trunks of the trees were visible now. I stared until the tree trunks glowed briefly like green flames. A wind blew through, making the green flames quiver—and I was where I wanted to be, standing before a stone farmhouse with candlelight shining softly through the windows.

Judgment

EELIE

The tall oaks towered above me, and the night wind rattled the dry leaves. It was April in Erland, but here in Midgard it was October already, and the fallen leaves smelled sweet in the darkness. I still had this one thing to do before I could go back to Castle Ellorgore.

Inside the stone farmhouse I saw Bab Magga moving about, her shadow moving with her across the walls. She carried a lighted candle over to the table and opened a big black book. I could see in my mind the pages of the book as she turned them, searching for a certain formula. The book held some Power, but also a vast jumble of worthless nonsense. The pages with Power crackled, but it was like the small fitful flame burning in a pile of dried leaves. Bab Magga felt the Power in the book—I could tell by the reverent way she turned the pages—but she seemed unable to tell where the Power was and where it wasn't.

I stood outside the window watching her, considering how to approach her. Raekkin had taught me that the approach was everything—as in hunting: it mattered whether you came from upwind or downwind. I knew that Clootie was the go-between, and I knew exactly how Clootie talked and looked. As I thought about Clootie, I knew I must come as a jackdaw, as like Clootie as a twin. It felt very small to be a jackdaw after being an eagle. I fluttered up to the windowsill and rapped on the glass with my beak.

Bab Magga looked up and saw me. She closed the book carefully and came to let me in.

"Ah, dear Jack," she said, "so you've come at last, and almost a stranger! I've been needing your help badly."

I bowed briskly and flew over to the table. I looked around at all the horrors she had hanging about the room. It was worse than Owen's description. I cocked one eye at the book and laughed Clootie's high, malicious laugh. "Japes and vanities!" I said mockingly. "Claptrap, hokum, hocus-pocus. It won't any of it help you, Bab Magga. You're in worse trouble than you know!"

"None of your jokes," she said. "If I'm in trouble, tell me right out. Don't go beating about the bush."

That struck me as funny. "The bush! A bird in the bush! That's what your Eben is now. He's no longer a bird in the hand—and perhaps he's no longer a goat." I watched her carefully to see her reaction.

She laughed. "That can't be," she said. "Even if he's run off to Rowan Tree Island, where I can't work magic to bring him back, he'll never be able to cast off my spell. You told me so yourself when you gave me the Power Charm. Or was I wrong to believe you, Jack?"

That was what I needed to know. I needed to know where her Power Charm was hidden.

"I told you the truth," I said in the jackdaw's high voice.

213

"Jack's not a liar! But do you have your Power Charm now, Bab Magga? Perhaps it's been stolen!"

Her hand slid to her throat and hesitated there. "No!" she said, her eyes narrowing. "No, I still have it!"

"You just think you have it. If it's been stolen, then the spell has been broken and Eben is no longer a goat. He's a man again—a man again! Ah, he's a fine man, isn't he, Bab Magga? But he's not yours any more. It might be that Owen has stolen your Power Charm."

"Owen!" she cried. "Owen! That's impossible. How could that brat steal it? He'd never dare. He'd never be able to come near me!"

"He might have had help."

"What sort of help?"

"Nora would help him."

"Nora! Now I know you're teasing me. You're wicked, Jack, indeed you are, to try to torment me. Ah, but I'll forgive you. Nora, indeed! What would Nora know about my spells or how to undo them?"

"She might have learned. She might have learned magic in Erland. Do you think she could stay there eleven years and not learn magic? And now she's home again, Bab Magga. She's come home."

"They'd never let her go!"

"Why not? Our Prince doesn't need her any more. So she's free, and she's come home, and she'd be the one who would help Owen steal your Power Charm!"

Bab Magga's hand went in then, into the neck of her gown, and she pulled out the small dark tangled knot that hung on a cord around her neck. I could feel the malignant Power in it, and so could she, for she laughed aloud.

"I've lost it, have I? Here it is, and it's still got its Power! I'll let it teach you a lesson, Jack! You need to learn respect."

She pulled the cord off over her head and flung the charm

down on the table. I jumped back, for I could feel the deadliness of it. Exactly what it was I did not know; but as I watched, the dark knot began to untie, to uncoil itself, to come to life, and slowly it turned blood red. A small snake head rose and flickered its tongue at me. That was what it had been all along—a bright red snake, dried and nowed into a tight knot. It seemed small, very small, to be so deadly. I did not dare take my eye off it. Could I seize it with my beak and kill it?

But even as I considered this, I realized it was too late. The snake was growing, getting larger—too large for a jackdaw. It coiled up on itself, hissing viciously. I just managed to jump back in time as it struck. I pecked at it hard, and it drew back, hissing. Then, faster than I could see, it whipped out again and coiled about my feet. It was even larger now. I flapped my wings, but I could not pull free. I had the horrible feeling that I was trapped. There was no time to think. I *changed* swifter than thought. I was an eagle, not a jackdaw, and the coiling red snake was wound about my talons.

I opened my hooked beak and snapped its head off. For a second I held the head in my beak, then I swallowed it. I felt the snake's head burning like a live coal as it slid down my throat. It continued burning inside me, and I felt its Power spreading through me. I was stronger now than ever before. I stood there on the table, my great wings half opened, still clutching the writhing body of the snake as it slowly faded and turned black and shriveled up.

"The spell is broken!" I said in my deep eagle's voice. "Eben is free now. Your Power is gone."

I raised the crest on my head and glared at Bab Magga with my fierce eagle eyes, and she shrank back, as shriveled and powerless as the dried snake's body.

"Who are you?" she whispered. "You're not Clootie!"

"No. I am Prince Elver of Erland. I am the baby that Nora raised. I am King of Erland now, and I order you to be quiet while I decide what to do with you. You deserve to be punished!"

The fear was plain in Bab Magga's eyes. "What have I done wrong?" she asked. "What harm have I done you?"

"You've done wrong to Nora and to Owen and to Eben! *But I told you to be quiet!*"

There was a silence between us until she could bear it no longer.

"What will it be then?" she asked in a terrified whisper.

So I pronounced judgment.

"You will live eleven years as a snake for the wrong you did Nora, eleven years as a three-legged cat for the wrong you did Owen, and eleven years as a goat for the wrong you did Eben. That is my judgment on you."

"Ah! And what of the good I did *you*? I sent Nora to you when you needed her to give you a chance to live. You owe your life to me! What reward will you give me for that?"

Bab Magga was like the snake; she could strike back. She had courage to ask me that, and I was forced to consider it. There was some justice in her statement. It had not been to save my life that she had sent Nora to Erland, but it was true that without Nora I would not have lived. I decided what would be fair.

"If you do no harm in all the years you spend as a snake and a cat and a goat—if you do no harm to anyone in all that time— then I will let you come to Erland where you can learn real sorcery. But you will never be able to come back here again. That is all I can offer you."

"That's fair enough," she said. "I'll wait gladly. I'll wait as a snake and a cat and a goat, and I'll be glad of the chance you're giving me."

But that wasn't the last of it. "What about Clootie?" she asked. "What punishment will Clootie have? He had a part in this, too!"

I glared at her; there was no end to her twistings and turnings. "Clootie obeyed his Queen," I said impatiently. "He did no wrong in that. But for the wrong he did Nora, which you know nothing about, and for his betrayal of my trust—he will be punished. But Clootie is an Erlander, and his punishment is not for you to understand."

Those were the last words I spoke, for I did not want to waste time arguing with her. I gave a flap of my great wings and was about to glide out the window when I glanced back and saw a snake go wriggling across the floor. That was Bab Magga, and I thought it better not to leave her there. Nora and Owen and Eben would be coming home soon, and Bab Magga might forget her good intentions. I turned back and picked her up in my talons.

"Stop squirming," I said, for she was writhing with fright. "I'm taking you away, for I don't trust you here."

I flew far through the black night, high over farms and woods and rivers, until, as the stars were fading in the lightening sky, I saw below a rocky and desolate land. I swept in low and dropped the snake there in that barren desert.

I flew back through the dawn sky, and as I flew over the farm, I saw, below, the white horse Ornhest approaching and on his back three people—Owen in front, then Eben, and then Nora.

I was happy for them, but I did not fly down to them. I made a low sweep over their heads and saw them look up with wonder, for they did not know me. Then I turned and headed out over the ocean.

The Dark Horn

EELIE

The sea stretched below me, the black waves tipped with flickering flame, as the sun rose like a ball of red fire and the night rolled back below the western horizon. I was flying, filled with triumph and delight. The feeling of flight was still a joy to me. My great wings swept me forward through the air, but a strong wind was blowing from the northeast. The clouds, flowing like fire, swept by, racing across the sky ahead of that wind. The wind rose higher and kept forcing me off my course. I kept fighting all day long against the force of that northland gale. It was hard to fly so far and so long with the wind against me. I was growing weary, and I found myself sinking lower, down, down toward the great rolling surface of the sea. I should have chosen to make the journey as a fish, but I had been entranced with the delight of flying, and I could not think fish thoughts enough to change now. I could only struggle to stay aloft.

But as I sank lower and lower until the salt spray was wetting my wing feathers—suddenly I saw Ornhest coming, skimming over the waves, neighing, calling to me. I could have cried aloud with joy at seeing him. I turned to meet him and came sweeping in, braking my weary wings to land safely on his back. And then I was glad to be myself again, no longer an eagle. It was a relief to sit there, safe in the saddle, as Ornhest galloped up and down the great heaving hills of the sea. He galloped as if on solid earth, and when his hoofs struck the waves they clanged like stone.

I leaned close to his neck and urged him on. "Faster!" I cried. "Fly, Ornhest, fly!" But he did not fly, though I knew he could. I could not remember the signal—I knew there was a signal to make him fly. Then I reminded myself of the dark horn that hung fastened to the saddle by a golden chain—the horn I had warned Nora not to touch. I reached for the horn and raised it to my lips. I drew in a great breath of air and blew—one long resounding blast.

Ornhest sprang into the air. He flashed like a streak of white light through the sky. And behind us, as thunder trails the lightning, the Hounds of the Wind came baying!

The heavens opened before us and split in two. The whole sky *turned inside out*, as the ravens had on the night of the Queen's Departing. Great walls of light rolled across the eastern sky, and waves of darkness rushed to meet them. They met with a great crash—louder than any thunder. The light and the dark shattered into fragments. The bits of white light fell in showers around us and the black light like sharp splinters of black glass.

But we rushed on so swiftly that I had no time for wonder. All around us there were clashing and rushing wind and galloping horses. The Choosers of the Slain came riding, and the Heroes—and there, careening across the heavens, I saw the

Chariot of the Moon overtaking and passing the Chariot of the Sun, and, in their passing, the sun turned black as coal with only a bright rim like a wheel of spinning light whirling through the eerie twilight sky. Overhead, high in the deep foreboding vastness of space, the stars of night came alight in countless galaxies.

Ornhest sprang upon the Wheel of the Sun, and we, too, went spinning dizzily through space. From all sides winged demons came flocking, swooping and hurtling through the air about us—wyverns, basilisks, and chimeras, and all the Thousand Beasts of Mystery. They spun, swirling like sparks in a great wind. I, too, felt all alight—my head was a ball of fire and my eyes were aflame. Ornhest was pale lightning streaming through the heavens. I shouted aloud, filled with exhilaration and a mad joy. We were beyond Fire and Ice, far in the Twilight of Time, and the whole sky was ours!

Then Skol, Hati, and Maanagram, the great gray wolves of the Twilight, arose and came howling after us, but the Hounds of the Wind turned upon them. I heard the belling of the pack as they swept off, far off, into the distance.

But the fire of my excitement was dying. My head was growing weary and drooping low, until I lay with my face pressed close against Ornhest's massive neck. I heard the baying hounds drawing near again, and their yelping chorus repeated my own name over and over, "Hjälper, Hjälper, Hjälper. . . ." My eyes were heavy, and as I closed them, I heard a voice command, *"Take my son home, Ornhest!"*

I opened my eyes and saw a great Spirit Wolf racing along beside us. I could only smile to see him there.

I closed my eyes again and laid my head on the great white billowing mane.

Author's Note

This novel is a work of imagination, but it includes folklore elements from traditional English-Scottish ballads and Norse mythology. For the benefit of those interested in folklore, these are some of the sources I have used:

The basic inspiration for this story comes from ballad #40, "The Queen of Elfan's Nourice," in Francis James Child's collection *The English and Scottish Popular Ballads*. This is really only a ballad fragment, but even in its fragmentary state it has great power to capture the imagination.

Chapter 30 is based on another Child ballad: #4, "Lady Isabel and the Elf Knight." I have made a free combination of the many versions discussed by Professor Child and added some new twists of my own. The first doves' song is adapted from this same source.

The taunting verses in Chapter 3 are revised and adapted

from a ballad, "The Queen of Sluts," which derives from "Kempy Kay," #33 in Child's collection.

The song "The Castle of Dromore" is adapted from a nine-teenth-century Irish lullaby.

The song "The River of Flowers" in Chapter 15 is my own, but is inspired by a verse from a very old French folk song, sung to me by Kate Barnes, which translates, "In the middle of the bed the river is deep / All the horses of the King come there to drink together." The original French song may be found in *Le Livre des Chansons* by H. Davenson, pp. 321–323.

The Harper's songs in Chapter 28 are my own, except for the first verse of the second song, which is adapted from a poem written by my father. The song the Harper sings in Chapter 30 is a fragment of an Appalachian song based on Child ballad #76, "The Lass of Roch Royal."

The ravens' song in Chapter 21, the second doves' song in Chapter 30, the song of the rowan trees in Chapter 14, as well as the "runes" or "charm songs," are all my own.

The various elements of Norse mythology derive from tradi-tional sources. "Wheeltide" is the winter solstice, which merged into the Christian Yuletide, deriving from the Old Norse word *hjöl*, meaning "wheel." The flaming wheel represented the sun on its journey through the sky; the ceremony celebrated the "rebirth" of the sun after its "death" on the eve of the longest night of the year.